Henry J. Jennings

Cardinal Newman

The Story of his Life. Second Edition

Henry J. Jennings

Cardinal Newman
The Story of his Life. Second Edition

ISBN/EAN: 9783744708050

Printed in Europe, USA, Canada, Australia, Japan

Cover: Foto ©Raphael Reischuk / pixelio.de

More available books at **www.hansebooks.com**

CARDINAL NEWMAN:

THE STORY OF HIS LIFE.

CARDINAL NEWMAN:

THE STORY OF HIS LIFE.

BY

HENRY J. JENNINGS,

AUTHOR OF "CURIOSITIES OF CRITICISM," ETC.

---

*" Newman has been the voice of the intellectual reaction of Europe, which was alarmed by an era of revolutions, and is looking for safety in the forsaken beliefs of the ages which it has been tempted to despise."—*J. A. FROUDE.

SECOND EDITION.

BIRMINGHAM:
HOUGHTON AND CO., SCOTLAND PASSAGE.
LONDON:
SIMPKIN, MARSHALL AND CO.

1882.

PREFATORY NOTE.

THE fact that I am not a Roman Catholic does not, I hope, disqualify me for attempting to sketch, however imperfectly, the career of a great dignitary of the Roman Church. I have endeavoured to write Cardinal Newman's Life without, on the one hand, concealing my own views, or, on the other, expressing them so as to give offence to those Catholics into whose hands the book may fall.

HENRY J. JENNINGS.

Handsworth Wood,
    Birmingham.

CONTENTS.

a Sketch from Memory
1841

CARDINAL NEWMAN.

CHAPTER I.

JOHN HENRY NEWMAN is one of the most remarkable men of the present century. He is remarkable both on account of his great intellectual gifts, and on account of the vicissitudes of his long and eventful career. During the best part of threescore years he has been at all times a notable factor in the history of the religious movements of the age. Mr. Austin, an acute critic, has accurately described him as "the man in the working of whose individual mind the intelligent portion of the English public is more interested than in that of any other living person." Whether as Oxford preacher, or Anglican reformer, or Tractarian disputant, or Catholic controversialist, or Roman Cardinal, he has continually filled a large place in popular interest. Whatever people may have thought of his creed, they have never had two opinions about his vast mental endowments. In him intellectual subtlety is combined with a rare profundity of learning. As theologian, dialectician, philosopher, historian, critic, poet, and preacher he has made a great and enduring mark. Skilful in controversy, earnest in all matters of belief, pure and high-minded in every action of his life, sincere when the world, with all the captiousness of the *odium theologicum*, deemed him insincere, he has filled with a noble record the long chapter of his fourscore years. To most Englishmen his features, through the agency of the camera, are familiar enough. They will readily recall his keen, ascetic face, as aquiline in character as that of the great Condé—a face worn with the deep furrows of one who has thought much, and troubled much, and, perhaps, suffered much. Still more readily will they recall the various episodes of his life, —his early fame as a preacher ; his identification with a movement which was then thought, and is still thought by many, to have had for its effect, whatever may have been its aim, the introduction of a Romanising spirit into the Church of England ; his ultimate secession to Rome ; his influence over a large body of waverers when the Catholic fever was at its height ; his controversies ; the honours conferred upon him in his old age ; and his quiet, sequestered, lettered life at the Edgbaston Oratory. They will recall, too,

how the sense of bitterness caused by his secession,—
the sense of betrayal, so to speak,—long since gave way
to a feeling of respectful confidence when his true
character was laid bare, and the world came to recognise
that every action of his life had been inspired by the
deepest and holiest convictions of conscience. It is
not necessary that one should be a communicant in the
Church of Rome to cherish an admiration bordering on
reverence for the eminent Oratorian. No man in this
world—not even the self-mortifying saints of the
Roman hagiology—ever led a holier life, in the sense
of purity, and piety, and devotional earnestness, and
conscientious zeal. Few men have ever handled the
weapons of polemical warfare with a more consummate
skill. Not very many have rivalled him in the
productiveness of his intellectual life, or in the variety
of his intellectual gifts.

It is of this distinguished man that I propose to give
a short sketch in the following pages. In doing so, a
controversial tone will be as much as possible avoided.
There is no need for the narrator to mix himself up
with the passions of a bygone period, or to identify
himself with the partisans of a particular creed. Nor
will the sketch make any pretensions to furnish new
and hitherto unpublished material. When Cardinal
Newman's biography comes to be fully written, as no
doubt it will be by some of those with whom he has
spent so many years in fraternal intercourse at the
Oratory, the materials for estimating his work will
probably be richer than they are now. As it is, I

pretend to no more than to compress into a brief narrative what is publicly known about the main facts of a very remarkable life.

John Henry Newman was born in London, in the year 1801. He was a son of Mr. John Newman, a member of the banking firm of Ramsbottom, Newman and Co. His younger brother, Francis, starting from the same point, and influenced at the outset by much the same training, arrived at conclusions diametrically opposed to his own. While the one drifted to religious liberalism, to pure Theism in fact, the mind of the other was gradually schooled to the opposite pole of Faith. How the result came about in the case of the more celebrated of the two we shall see by-and-bye. Of John's early life little is known except what he has told us himself, and that little has chiefly to do with his religious views. During the early part of his childhood he lived with his father in Bloomsbury Square. It is not a little remarkable that one of his early playmates should have been Benjamin Disraeli. According to the *Catholic Times*, " on most Saturday afternoons in the last year of the first decade of the present century two boys, aged respectively nine and five, might have been seen playing in the gardens of Bloomsbury Square, London. The boys, both natives of the Square, offered the most complete contrast to each other in appearance. The younger, whose head was profuse with long black glossy ringlets, was a child of rare Jewish type of beauty, and full of life and activity. The other was grave in demeanour, and wore his hair close cut, and walked and talked and moved in a way which in young people is called ' old-fashioned.' He was of pure English race and Puritan family. The names of the children denoted these differences as much as their appearances. The one was Benjamin Disraeli, the other John Newman." Both of these lads had a great future before them : one becoming Prime Minister of Great Britain, and the other a Roman Cardinal. Young Newman was brought up from a child to take great delight in reading the Bible. A child's love for the Bible depends very much on the manner in which he is introduced to it. If it be made a penal book, or even an ordinary lesson book,—if the child has to read out of it as part of his daily task and to learn portions of it by heart when he has been naughty, then the chances are that he will grow up, if not positively to hate it, yet blind to the charm of its narrative, the richness of its imagery, the glow and loftiness of its poetry, and the comfort of its truths. When Newman tells us that he was brought up to take great delight in reading the Bible, we may be sure that the delight sprang from methods of a very different kind from those which obtain in families where the Scriptures are austerely crammed down the throats of the youngsters. He formed no religious convictions till he was fifteen. He remembered wishing that the Arabian tales were true, and his mind ran on unknown influences, on magical powers, and talismans. He thought life might be a dream, and he an angel, and all this world a deception. These were remarkable imaginings for so young a mind. A taste for the mysterious, for the·

supernatural, for the occult, is not altogether phenomenal in early boyhood, especially in the case of boys with the imaginative faculty vigorously developed ; but it rarely takes such strange and mystic shapes as young Newman experienced. He was " very superstitious," and used to cross himself on going into the dark. In one of his school copy-books he drew a solid upright cross and a string of beads. He was not clear how these symbols of Rome got into his head, but supposed that he got the idea from some romance,—Mrs. Radcliffe's or Miss Porter's,—or some religious picture. There was nothing in the churches he attended, or the prayer-books he used, to suggest them. The fact, after all, is of no great importance. Hundreds of boys draw crosses and beads, who are as little under the influence of Roman methods as he was at that time. Probably he was as little moved by the subject of this early draughtsmanship as nine hundred and ninety-nine schoolboys out of every thousand would be. At the age of fourteen, he read Paine's Tracts against the Old Testament, and " found pleasure " in thinking of the objections that were contained in them. He also read some of Hume's Essays, perhaps that on Miracles ; so at least he gave his father to understand, " but perhaps it was a brag." Here, at any rate, was evidence of a studious and contemplative turn. Paine and Hume are curious works for a boy to select at an age when *Robinson Crusoe*, or some narrative of heroic deeds and stirring adventure, generally captivates the fancy. But Newman's was a precocious intellect,—

precocious only in the sense of being in advance of his years. It had none of the weakness and want of endurance which sometimes characterize minds of this class. When he was fifteen he fell under the influences of a definite creed, and received into his intellect—these are his own words—impressions of dogma. He read books of the school of Calvin, received the doctrine of final perseverance, believed in his own inward conversion, and that he was elected to eternal glory. The dominant faculty of his intelligence came thus early into play. The boy was a theologian even in his teens. At an age when most lads rarely trouble themselves about serious matters at all, or, if they do, care very little about the doctrinal basis of their belief, he was already studying grave problems of religion, isolating himself from surrounding objects, and confirming himself in his mistrust of the reality of material phenomena. He rested, he has told us, in the thought of two, and two only, supreme and luminously self-evident beings— himself and his Creator. Stronger influences began by-and-bye to assert themselves over his nature. A deep impression was made upon him by Thomas Scott, "to whom," he says, "(humanly speaking) I owe my soul," and whose "bold unwordliness and vigorous independence of mind" left visible impressions upon his plastic intelligence. Before he was sixteen he made a collection of Scripture texts in proof of the doctrine of the Trinity; and a few months later he arranged a series of texts in support of each verse of the Athanasian Creed. From this time he gave a full inward assent

and belief to the doctrine of eternal punishment, in as
true a sense as he held that of eternal happiness. Then,
he had been reading Milner's Church History, and had
been " nothing short of enamoured " of the long extracts
from St. Augustine and the other Fathers. He read,
too, Newton on the Prophecies, and was convinced that
the Pope was the Antichrist predicted by Daniel, St.
Paul, and St. John. His imagination, he tells us, was
" stained " by the effects of this doctrine until 1843, which
remained, even after it was obliterated from his reason,
as "a sort of false conscience." He was still only fifteen
when the idea possessed him that it was the will of God
he should lead a single life; that he ought to lead a
missionary life among the heathen, for which celibacy
would be a condition. It is almost amusing to think
of this mere lad taking such matters seriously into his
consideration at all.

A gap of six years occurs in the record which he has
left us. Meanwhile he had gone to a private school at
Ealing, and thence to Oxford, where he graduated
with classical honours in 1820, and was soon after
elected to a fellowship of Oriel. The influences under
which he was thus brought were of the most intellectual
kind. The fellowships of Oriel were open, and she was
able to draw to her some of the ablest men in the
University. The late Lord Grenville used to term an
Oriel Fellowship at this time the Blue Ribbon of the
University, and the distinction attained by such men as
Hawkins, Davison, Keble, Whately, Arnold, Pusey,
Newman, Hurrell Froude, and the Wilberforces was a

fair justification of the metaphor. Newman was thus introduced to a society leavened with the most intellectual influences, and animated by a spirit of inquiry above mere scholarship. It is questionable, perhaps, whether the supreme contempt evinced by the guiding minds of Oriel for mundane honours tended to raise the academic tone of the college. The brilliant galaxy of Fellows had its disadvantages as well as its advantages, and the scholarship of the students was apt to suffer through the want of a more practical government. Mr. Newman's academical career assumed at once, both on account of his splendid gifts as well as through the associations of Oriel, the promise of conspicuous brilliancy. University tradition tells of his wide scholarship, his omnivorous reading, his retentive memory, and his clear, methodical intellect. In 1822 he fell under different influences from those to which he had hitherto been subjected. Dr. Whately, and Dr. Hawkins, then Vicar of St. Mary's, began to give him new ideas and instil into him new phases of thought. The latter taught him to weigh his words and be cautious in his statements; and gave him some of those "logical ideas" which were afterwards supposed by his opponents to savour of the polemics of Rome. Dr. Hawkins seems to have been a severe, but probably a just critic.

In 1824 Newman took orders and was appointed to a curacy in Oxford. His first sermon was preached from the text "Man goeth forth unto his work and to his labour until the evening." It

was not, perhaps, an altogether undesigned coincidence
that the last sermon he preached at St. Mary's,
before resigning the living in 1843, should have
been from the same text. As regards his earlier pulpit
efforts he had a candid friend in Dr. Hawkins, who
" snubbed " them and encouraged greater precision of
language. Before this, however, he lent Newman a
work which influenced him to give up his remaining
Calvinism and to receive the doctrines of Baptismal
Regeneration, and Tradition. He laid it down as a
principle that the sacred text was never intended to
teach doctrine, but only to prove it ; and that for
doctrine one must go to the formularies of the Church,
—the Catechism and the Creeds. Whately held the
same view. Newman adopted it, and one of its
consequences was to lead him to withdraw from the
Bible Society, at the root of whose principle it struck.
It is not necessary, however, to follow closely the
thread of Newman's own narrative as to the formation
of his religious opinions. We find that he was
brought more directly into Whately's companionship
by being appointed, in 1825, Vice-Principal of St.
Alban's Hall, of which the latter was at the head. At
one time he found himself drifting in the direction of
Liberalism, and using " flippant language against the
Fathers." Four years later, however, he formally broke
with Whately, having been recalled to his former
condition of mind by two great blows—illness and
bereavement. In 1826 he was made tutor of Oriel,
an office which he held until 1831. The way in which

he discharged the functions of this responsible post may be guessed from a remark which he let fall many years later in addressing a deputation which had come to congratulate him on some special occasion. He said then that the teaching of classics did not absolve the tutor from the responsibility of imparting an ethical training. " I consider," he added, " the college tutor to have a care of souls."

In 1827, so high was his distinction as a ripe scholar that he was appointed one of the Examiners for the B.A. degree. Nor was his knowledge confined to academical subjects. He read omnivorously, and " studied modern thought and modern life—in all its forms, and with all its many-coloured passions." " Newman's mind," says Mr. J. A. Froude, " was world-wide. He was interested in everything which was going on in science, in politics, in literature. Nothing was too large for him, nothing too trivial, if it threw light upon the central question, what man really was, and what was his destiny. He was careless about his personal prospects. He had no ambition to make a career, or to rise to rank and power. Still less had pleasure any seductions for him. His natural temperament was bright and light; his senses, even the commonest, were exceptionally delicate. I was told that, though he rarely drank wine, he was trusted to choose the vintages for the college cellar. He could admire enthusiastically any greatness of action and character, however remote the sphere of it from his own. Gurwood's 'Dispatches of the Duke of

Wellington' came out just then. Newman had been
reading the book, and a friend asked him what he
thought of it. 'Think?' he said, 'it makes one burn to
have been a soldier!'"

The same writer, whose sketch of Dr. Newman in
Good Words attracted considerable interest on its
appearance, also gives the following particulars of his
University life:—"He seemed always to be better
informed on common topics of conversation than any
one else who was present. He was never condescending
with us (undergraduates), never didactic or authoritative;
but what he said carried conviction along with it.
When we were wrong he knew why we were wrong,
and excused our mistakes to ourselves while he set us
right. Perhaps his supreme merit as a talker was that
he never tried to be witty or to say striking things.
Ironical he could be, but not ill-natured. Not a
malicious anecdote was ever heard from him. Prosy he
could not be. He was lightness itself—the lightness of
elastic strength—and he was interesting because he
never talked for talking's sake, but because he had
something real to say . . . . The simplest word
which dropped from him was treasured as if it had been
an intellectual diamond. For hundreds of young men
Credo in Newmannum was the genuine symbol of
faith."

Prior to this, however, he had attained some
distinction as a writer. In 1830, a proposal was made
to him to contribute a work to a Theological Library
then in course of formation. The outcome of this

invitation was the "History of the Arians." Up to this time, Newman had, according to a trustworthy authority, half resolved to give himself to science and mathematics. The tendency of his new studies, however, was to determine him to a theological career. Ecclesiastical history appears to have had from the first a peculiar fascination for him, and its influence is traceable in much of his subsequent conduct.

He formed during this period intimacies of an enduring and influential kind with Pusey and Keble. In 1828 he received the incumbency of St. Mary's Church, with the outlying chaplaincy of Littlemore, and this he held till 1843. His appearance about this time is graphically described by the contemporary observer already quoted. " He was above the middle height, slight and spare. His head was large, his face remarkably like that of Julius Cæsar. The forehead, the shape of the ears and nose were almost the same. The lines of the mouth were very peculiar, and I should say exactly the same. I have often thought of the resemblance, and believed that it extended to the temperament. In both there was an original force of character which refused to be moulded by circumstances, which was to make its own way, and become a power in the world ; a clearness of intellectual perception, a disdain for conventionalities, a temper imperious and wilful, but along with it a most attaching gentleness, sweetness, singleness of heart and purpose. Both were formed by nature to command others, both had the faculty of attracting to themselves the passionate devotion of their friends and followers, and in both cases, too, perhaps the devotion was rather due to the personal ascendancy of the leader than to the cause which he represented. It was Cæsar, not the principle of the empire, which overthrew Pompey and the constitution. *Credo in Newmannum* was a common phrase at Oxford, and is still unconsciously the faith of nine-tenths of the English converts to Rome."

Newman soon gained a reputation as a preacher. His style was wonderfully lucid, his language coloured with the rich glows of a picturesque imagination. Of action and dramatic effect he had none ; he read his sermons with his eyes fixed for the most part on his manuscript, but what he lacked in the Demosthenic qualification of an orator he made up for in a voice of singular and persuasive sweetness. Mr. Gladstone has described the impression left upon his mind by Newman's preaching, about 1837. "Dr. Newman," he said, in a speech on Preaching, delivered at the City Temple in 1877, "when I was an undergraduate at Oxford, was looked upon rather with prejudice as what is termed a Low Churchman, but was very much respected for his character and his known ability. He was then vicar of St. Mary's at Oxford, and used to preach there. Without ostentation or effort, but by simple excellence he was constantly drawing undergraduates more and more around him. Now, Dr. Newman's manner in the pulpit was one about which, if you considered it in its separate parts, you would arrive at very unsatisfactory conclusions. There was not very much change in the inflexion of the voice; action there was none. His sermons were read, and his eyes were always bent on his book, and all that, you will say, is against efficiency in preaching. Yes, but you take the man as a whole, and there was a stamp and a seal upon him; there was a solemn sweetness and music in the tone; there was a completeness in the figure, taken together with the tone and with the manner, which made even his delivery, such as I have described it, and though exclusively from written sermons, singularly attractive." "No one," says Mr. J. A. Froude, " who heard his sermons in those days can ever forget them. They were seldom directly theological. We had theology enough and to spare from the select preachers before the university. Newman, taking some Scripture character for a text, spoke to us about ourselves, our temptations, our experiences. His illustrations were inexhaustible. He seemed to be addressing the most secret consciousness of each of us—as the eyes of a portrait appear to look at every person in a room. He never exaggerated; he was never unreal. A sermon from him was a poem, formed on a distinct idea, fascinating by its subtlety, welcome—how welcome!—from its sincerity, interesting from its originality, even to those who were careless of religion; and to others who wished to be religious, but had found religion dry and wearisome, it was like the springing of a fountain out of the rock." Mr. Froude, by way of illustrating Newman's powers as a preacher, relates that on one occasion he described closely some of the incidents of our Lord's passion; then he paused.

"For a few moments there was a breathless silence. Then, in a low, clear voice, of which the faintest vibration was audible in the farthest corner of St. Mary's, he said, ' Now, I bid you recollect that He to whom these things were done was Almighty God.' It was as if an electric stroke had gone through the church, as if every person present understood for the first time the meaning of what he had all his life been saying. I suppose it was an epoch in the mental history of more than one of my Oxford contemporaries."

The testimony of his then contemporaries is more valuable than anything else in helping us, at a distance of so many years, to comprehend the fascinations of Mr. Newman's pulpit style. Another of these contemporaries was Mr. Oakeley, who in his *Notes on the Tractarian Movement* gives the following graphic picture of the leader of the party. "The service (at St. Mary's), like its companion in the forenoon, was conducted entirely by Mr. Newman, who had succeeded, in his turn, as Fellow of Oriel, to the incumbency of the parish Mr. Newman was, in fact, everything in this office—alike without rival and without coadjutor ; he was reader, preacher, and celebrant ; nay, music and ceremonial also ; for, if these various departments were ever actually filled by others, they have faded from the memory, which has settled down on him alone. It was from that pulpit that Sunday after Sunday were delivered those marvellous discourses which have been since collected into several volumes, and of which it may be said that there is hardly a sentence which does

not form a study for the philosopher.   Nor was it in
the pulpit alone that Mr. Newman had the gift of
throwing a character essentially his own over the work
in which he was engaged.   He succeeded in imparting
to the Anglican service, and especially to that portion
of it which from the lips of most clergymen was either
an unimpressive recital or a pompous effort—the
reading of the lessons—an indescribable charm of
touching beauty, and a wonderful power of instructive
efficacy.   His delivery of Scripture was a sermon in
which you forgot the human preacher; a drama in
which the vividness of the representation was marred
by no effort and degraded by no art.   He stood before
the sacred volume as if penetrating its contents to their
very centre, so that his manner alone, his pathetic
changes of voice, or his thrilling pauses, seemed to
convey the commentary in the simple enunciation of
the text.   He brought out meanings where none had
been even suspected, and invested passages which in
the hands of the profane are often the subject of
unbecoming levity, with a solemnity which forced
irreverence to retire abashed into its hiding-places."

CHAPTER II.

THE TRACTARIAN MOVEMENT—HOSTILITY TO RELIGIOUS LIBERALISM
—ORIGIN OF THE MOVEMENT—HURRELL FROUDE—NEWMAN'S
ILLNESS IN SICILY—"LEAD, KINDLY LIGHT"—KEBLE'S
INFLUENCE—THE "CHRISTIAN YEAR"—NEWMAN, THE INTEL-
LECTUAL LEADER—"TRACTS FOR THE TIMES"—THE "VIA
MEDIA"—HAMPDEN'S APPOINTMENT—"TRACT XC"—ITS
EFFECT IN OXFORD—ACTION OF THE HEBDOMADAL COUNCIL—
PRECIPITANCY OF CONDEMNATION—DISCONTINUANCE OF THE
TRACTS—COLLISION WITH THE NATION—LITERARY ACTIVITY—
NEWMAN AND THE "TIMES."

THE history of the Tractarian movement has been so
often and so ably told that it will not be necessary to
give more than an outline of it in the present volume.
It was far different in its origin from its ultimate
development. There was no thought of the *Via Media*
at the outset. The views of its leaders, or at least of
some of them, grew bolder in the course of the eight
years or so of their activity. It was considered
imperative by a handful of zealous young Oxford men,
in 1833, that something should be done to stem the tide
of religious liberalism that seemed to be making
headway. The anti-dogmatic principle was gaining
ground. Apprehensions were excited that the Church
was in danger of destruction. It is a significant
circumstance that the High Church revival began in
less than a twelvemonth from the passing of the Reform

Bill, and the suppression of two archbishoprics and eight bishoprics in Ireland. It is impossible to divest it altogether of a political character. Its founders fancied that a great and united effort was needed to check the radical tendencies of the times. Lord Grey had recommended the bishops to put their house in order. "The vital question," as Newman put it, was " how are we to keep the Church from being liberalized ? "

What he meant by Liberalism he has explained in a note to the later editions of the *Apologia.* "It means," he says, "false liberty of thought, or the exercise of thought upon matters in which, from the constitution of the human mind, thought cannot be brought to any successful issue, and therefore is out of place." The school of anti-dogmatic theology which excited this animosity numbered amongst its foremost men Dr. Arnold of Rugby, and Dr. Whately. It was, in fact, the nucleus of that intellectual movement which later on developed into the Broad Church party, and influenced in so great a degree the religious tendencies of the age. Newman and his friends were angered by the spirit that was abroad, and they entered upon the work of its destruction with unforbearing zeal. It was subsequently their fate to be discomfited by the allies of this same party. Newman's feelings towards the Liberals, whom he subsequently charged with having " driven him from Oxford "—a charge which on mature consideration he found himself unable to modify—were expressed in a copy of verses written in 1833 in the *British Magazine*, and afterwards printed in the *Lyra Apostolica*.

Ye cannot halve the Gospel of God's grace ;
Men of presumptuous heart ! I know you well.
Ye are of those who plan that we should dwell,
   Each in his tranquil home and holy place ;
Seeing the Word refines all nature's rude,
And tames the stirrings of the multitude.

And ye have caught some echoes of its lore,
As heralded amid the joyous choirs ;
Ye mark'd it spoke of peace, chastised desires ;
   Good-will and mercy,—and ye heard no more ;
But, as for zeal and quick-eyed sanctity,
And the dread depths of grace, ye pass'd them by.

And so ye halve the Truth ; for ye in heart,
At best, are doubters whether it be true,
The theme discarding, as unmeet for you,
   Statesmen or Sages.   O new-compass'd art
Of the ancient Foe !—but what, if it extends
O'er our own camp, and rules amid our friends !

Similar thoughts had taken deep root in the minds of Arthur Perceval, Hurrell Froude, and William Palmer, three young men of high character and promise, who, in the month of July, consulted with the Rev. Hugh James Rose, editor of the *British Magazine*, and subsequently Professor of Theology at Durham, Principal at King's College, London, and chaplain to the Archbishop of Canterbury.   Mr. Rose may in some sense be regarded as the real founder of the movement.   A conference was held at Hadleigh, at which it was resolved to unite the efforts of High Churchmen to maintain the doctrine of Apostolic Succession, and preserve the Prayer Book from Socinian adulterations. Newman, who was travelling on the Continent while the first ideas of the party were shaping themselves to the aim of some definite action, shared the views of his Oxford friends. Hurrell Froude later on influenced his mind in the direction of views which were not in harmony with the Evangelical theory of the Church of England. "He made me," says Newman, "to look with admiration towards the Church of Rome, and in the same degree to dislike the Reformation. He fixed deep in me the idea of devotion to the Blessed Virgin, and he led me gradually to believe in the Real Presence." Froude was a young man of singular gifts and a powerful mind. Dr. Newman has given a Rembrandt portrait of him in the *Apologia.* "Hurrell Froude," he says, "was a pupil of Keble's, formed by him, and in turn reacting upon him. He was a man of the highest gifts, so truly many-sided that it would be presumptuous in me to attempt to describe him, except under those aspects in which he came before me. Nor have I here to speak of the gentleness and tenderness of nature, the playfulness, the free elastic force and graceful versatility of mind, and the patient winning considerateness in discussion which endeared him to those to whom he opened his heart; for I am all along engaged upon matters of belief and opinion, and am introducing others into my narrative, not for their own sakes, or because I love and have loved them, so much as because, and so far as, they have influenced my theological views. In this respect, then, I speak of Hurrell Froude—in his intellectual aspects—as a man of high genius, brimful and overflowing with ideas and views, in him original, which were too many and too strong even for his bodily strength, and which crowded and jostled against each other in their effort after distinct shape and impression ; and he had an intellect as critical and logical as it was speculative and bold. Dying prematurely, as he did, and in the conflict and transition-state of opinion, his religious views never reached their ultimate conclusion, by the very reason of their multitude and depth. His opinions arrested and influenced me, even when they did not gain my assent. . . . . He had a keen insight into abstract truth ; but he was an Englishman to the backbone in his severe adherence to the real and the concrete. He had a most classical taste, and a genius for philosophy and art ; and he was fond of historical inquiry, and the politics of religion. He had no turn for theology as such. He had no appreciation of the writings of the Fathers, of the details or development of doctrine, of the definite traditions of the Church viewed in their matter, of the teaching of the Ecumenical Councils, or of the controversies out of which they arose. He took an eager, courageous view of things on the whole. I should say that his power of entering into the minds of others did not equal his other gifts ; he could not believe, for instance, that I really held the Roman Church to be Anti-Christian." Hurrell Froude's influence upon Newman was of

Lead, kindly Light, amid the encircling gloom,
Lead Thou me on!

The night is dark, and I am far from home —
Lead Thou me on!

Keep Thou my feet; I do not ask to see
The distant scene, — one step enough for me.

I was not ever thus, nor prayed that Thou
Shouldst lead me on.

I loved to choose and see my path, but now

So long Thy power hath blest me, sure it still
Will lead me on, —
O'er moor and fen, o'er crag and torrent, till
The night is gone;
And with the morn those Angel faces smile
Which I have loved long since, and lost awhile!

John H Newman

July 11. 1874

a powerful kind. The views which he led him to adopt, and the additions which he was the means of contributing to his theological creed, were not, however, the immediate outcome of their friendship; nor were feelings so strong the ostensible cause of the Tractarian movement. When Newman compared the Church of his day with the vigorous power she had displayed in the first centuries, he felt, he tells us, dismay at her prospects, anger and scorn at her do-nothing perplexity. The vital principle which actuated the plan for united effort was that there was "need of a second Reformation." There was a "National Apostacy" which *must* be counteracted.

On returning to England in July, full of fierce thoughts against the Liberals, whose success fretted him, he came as one impressed with the idea that he had a mission. This feeling, indeed, had haunted him abroad. When he lay ill of a fever in Sicily, he firmly believed that he should be spared for the work in England. "I have a work to do,—I have a work to do," he sobbed out in the weak moments of his convalescence. It was on his homeward journey that he wrote the well-known and beautiful hymn, "Lead, kindly Light." This journey had been fruitful in poetic inspiration. Newman, from the time he left Falmouth —December 13th, 1832,—to June 27th, 1833, when he was at Marseilles, on his way home, wrote in all seventy-nine poems, of which forty-three are stated to have been written "at sea," or "off" various places near which the vessel was lying. On six days he wrote two poems each day, and on five days he wrote three each day. From the 1st to the 13th of June ten poems are all dated from Palermo, and next in order comes " Lead, kindly Light," which was written "at sea" on the 16th, under the title of "The Pillar of the Cloud." Respecting this hymn some controversy has arisen of late years as to the meaning of the last two lines :—

"And with the morn those angel faces smile
Which I have loved long since, and lost awhile."

Dr. Newman on being himself applied to a year or two ago to explain exactly what was meant by these " angel faces," made the following reply :—

"The Oratory, January 18, 1879.

"My dear Mr. Greenhill,

"You flatter me by your question, but I think it was Keble who, when asked it in his own case, answered that poets were not bound to be critics, or to give a sense to what they had written ; and though I am not like him, a poet, at least I may plead that I am not bound to *remember* my own meaning, whatever it was, at the end of almost fifty years. Anyhow, there must be a statute of limitation for writers of verse, or it would be quite a tyranny if, in an art which is the expression not of truth but of imagination and sentiment, one were obliged to be ready for examination on the transient state of mind which came upon one when home-sick or sea-sick, or in any other way sensitive or excited.

"Yours most truly,
"JOHN H. NEWMAN"

This letter drew forth a number of replies in the pages of *Notes and Queries*, the chief points in discussion being the possible meanings which Dr. Newman may have intended at the time of writing, and his dictum that poetry is not expressive of truth. These literary curiosities must not, however, detain us by the way. When he reached home Newman threw himself at once and with ardour into the project to which Rose, and Hurrell Froude, and the others now stood committed. Keble, too, the author of the *Christian Year*, was of the party. Dr. Newman, indeed, assigns to him the most notable place in connection with the Tractarian movement. "In and from Keble," he says, "the mental activity of Oxford took the direction which issued in what was called Tractarianism,"—that is, an anti-Liberal direction. Keble had few sympathies with the intellectual party. "Poor Keble!" Hurrell Froude used gravely to say, "he was asked to join the aristocracy of talent, but he soon found his level." Yet he was to some extent instrumental in forming a school which had an instinctive hatred of "heresy, insubordination, resistance to things established, claims of independence, disloyalty, innovation, a critical, censorious spirit." This was probably due to the intensity of his prejudice,—one might, indeed, almost say of his narrowness. He was so bitterly opposed to anything in the shape of liberal opinions in theology that, one day, calling at a house where one of the family had imbibed those opinions, and learning that the offender was at home, he refused to enter, and remained sitting in the porch. He lent to the movement a savour of cautious orthodoxy which contributed to its toleration by men who

did not altogether relish the religious antecedents
of Dr. Pusey and Mr. Newman; and his *Christian
Year*, though it is not, in the opinion of some
critics, of a specially high order of poetry, had
done much to prepare the public mind for the
doctrines which were afterwards to be advocated by
the Tractarians. Dr. Newman says of this volume,
in one of his Essays, that "it was the most
soothing, tranquillising, subduing work of the day;
if poems can be found to enliven in dejection, and
to comfort in anxiety, to cool the over-sanguine,
to refresh the weary, and to awe the worldly; to
instil resignation into the impatient, and calmness
into the fearful and agitated—they are these."

On July 14th, Mr. Keble preached the Assize
Sermon in the University pulpit. The subject was
"National Apostacy," and Newman always set apart
that day as the start of the religious movement of
1833. But Newman, by the force of his great
gifts of scholarship, his commanding intellect, and
his signal courage, rose naturally into his place as
the intellectual leader of the party. Isaac Williams
and Dr. Pusey were also identified with the movement, but, like Keble and Froude, they fell into
secondary rank. "Compared with Newman they all
were but as ciphers, and he the indicating number."
It is important to bear this in mind in estimating
the extent and scope of Mr. Newman's influence.
Mr. J. A. Froude, Hurrell Froude's younger brother,
says, "The triumvirs who became a national force,

and gave its real character to the Oxford movement, were Keble, Pusey, and John Henry Newman.
Newman himself was the moving power; the two
others were powers also, but of inferior mental
strength. Without the third, they would have been
known as men of genius and learning; but their
personal influence would have been limited to and
have ended with themselves." So decisive were his
pretensions to the leadership of the party that
Bishop Blomfield made the characteristic jest that
"the whole movement was nothing but a Newmania."
It was considered desirable that the public should be
influenced by a literature specially directed to the
questions of Church reform which were now being
agitated. The *Tracts for the Times* were thereupon
started. At first they were, as the name implied, short
papers; later on they grew into elaborate treatises. It
was a cardinal point in the creed of the Tractarians
that the weakness of the Church was due to a want of
belief in her divine mission. They wanted to show
that she was not a mere act-of-parliament Church. In
the very first tract, which Newman wrote himself, the
question is put plainly, " On what are we to rest our
authority when the State deserts us ? " and the answer
is given as plainly, " On our Apostolical descent." The
authors of the tracts wanted, in fact, to show that the
Church was a body distinct from the State, and
capable of existing without its patronage and support.
It was, as an impartial writer has well said, a dream of
noble and generous minds. " They hoped to see the

Church under the divinely ordained government of bishops, priests, and deacons, not merely preaching the gospel and administering sacraments, but taking a high and independent stand, and exercising a profound influence on the religion and morality of the nation." The chief writers of the tracts besides Newman were Hurrell Froude, Pusey, and Isaac Williams. But almost from the first there were differences of opinion, and a want of unity. Palmer wanted the movement to be directed by a Committee or Association, and the Tracts, which Newman had begun "out of his own head," were looked upon by Palmer and his friends with alarm, inasmuch as they represented the antagonistic principle of personality. Keble and Froude, on the other hand, wanted the Tracts to go on. Gradually the aims of the more active spirits grew larger. They began to talk of the *Via Media.* There was a middle path, they thought, between the Protestant Church, as generally understood, and the Church of Rome. Newman was occupied for three years on a statement in support of this idea. He wrote it to show that he was opposed to Rome. When people said that what he and Froude were saying was "sheer Popery," he replied, "True, we seem to be making straight for it; but go on awhile, and you will come to a deep chasm across the path which makes real approximation impossible." The idea of an Anglican Church based on the principles of dogma,—a visible Church with sacraments and rites, "which are the channels of invisible grace,"—and holding to Authority and the worth of works of penance, was conceived to be possible without drifting too far in the direction of Popery. The new school discarded the Lutheran dictum that justification by faith only was the cardinal doctrine of Christianity, and Newman wrote an Essay in support of their view.

The conflict between the High Church party and the Broad Church party was accentuated in 1836 by the appointment of Dr. Hampden to the Regius Professorship of Divinity, on the nomination of Lord Melbourne. Four years previously Hampden had enunciated, in the Bampton Lectures, a theology which, although there was nothing particularly unorthodox in it, challenged the antagonism of Newman and his friends. His appointment was therefore made the ground of a sharp attack. Newman's searching critical power was brought to bear in a pamphlet entitled *Elucidations of the Bampton Lectures*, and the growing discontent, fanned somewhat by political passions, resulted in Convocation passing a vote of censure upon Dr. Hampden. Some twelve years later, when he was appointed to the Bishopric of Hereford, the controversy broke out with renewed bitterness, but Dr. Newman was then an uninterested spectator no longer connected with the Church of England, and Hampden himself rapidly subsided into theological insignificance, from which he never afterwards emerged.

The Tractarian movement, which it would take too much space to describe in detail, went on until it "came into collision with the nation." Alarm was fairly excited by the appearance of Tract LXXX. There had been a grave feeling of uneasiness before, but this particular treatise, which advocated "reserve" in communicating religious knowledge, provoked a serious outcry. The author of this, Mr. Isaac Williams, contended that the highest mysteries of religion should not be thrown down before the careless and indifferent. Probably he had no expectation of the interpretation that would be put upon his words. The term "reserve," was, indeed, a peculiarly unfortunate one. People jumped to the conclusion that the object of it was to keep back the most unpopular doctrines of Romanism till the public mind was prepared for them. A storm of disapprobation was aroused. It was thought that the Tractarians were bent on "Romanising" the Church, and that they meant to conceal the various stages of their insidious attempt. The conflict, however, did not come to a crisis just then. Ten more of the Tracts were issued before the voice of authority was raised against them, although Newman's on the "Breviary" had drawn down the remonstrances of Dr. Bagot, the Bishop of Oxford.

The fame of "Tract XC" has become historical. Its appearance was the acute crisis of the whole movement. The object with which it was written was the retention in the English Communion of members of the Church who were inclined to Rome. It aimed at showing that a clergyman could subscribe to the formularies and Articles of the Established Church, and yet hold almost all the Roman doctrines against which those articles

had hitherto been thought to be a protest. It maintained that the Thirty-nine Articles, although the
offspring of an uncatholic age, are, to say the least,
not uncatholic, and may be subscribed by those who
aim at being Catholic in heart and doctrine. Newman
was the author of this startling treatise, which acted
as the proverbial straw on the endurance of the
Protestant party. He argued his case with great skill.
He showed that the Articles were composed several
years before the canons of the Council of Trent were
published, and therefore could not have been intended
to contradict them; that they were not directed
against Catholic doctrines, but against the popular
abuses of them; and that they were legal documents
to be interpreted according to the strict meaning of
the words. He reached the conclusion that the Articles
did not condemn the authoritative teaching of the
Church of Rome on Purgatory, on the Invocation of
Saints, and on the Mass. Newman has given us a
frank statement of the intellectual processes which led
him to this result. He referred to the Homilies, and
endeavoured to show that their incorporation in the
Anglican system of doctrine could not have been made
by men governed by the existing clearly-marked lines
between Rome and Protestantism. It is, as Mr. Froude
says, historically certain that Elizabeth and her ministers
intentionally framed the Church formulas so as to
enable everyone to use them who would disclaim
allegiance to the Pope. "Newman was only claiming
a position for himself and his friends which had been

purposely left open when the constitution of the
Anglican Church was formed." The actual cause of
the treatise, Newman tells us, was the restless-
ness of those who neither liked the *Via Media*
nor his own strong judgment against Rome. "It
was thrown in our teeth, 'How can you
manage to sign the Articles? They are directly
against Rome.'" His attempt to show how the two
seemingly contradictory principles could be reconciled
was received with a storm of indignation. He was
"unprepared for the outbreak, and startled by its
violence." Canon Oakeley says that Tract XC had not
been out many days before Oxford was in a fever of
excitement. "It was bought with such avidity that
the very presses were taxed almost beyond their powers
to meet the exigencies of the demand. Edition followed
edition by days rather than by weeks; and it was not
very long before Mr. Newman, as I have heard, realised
money enough by the sale of this shilling pamphlet to
purchase a valuable library. If, during the month
which followed its appearance, you had happened to
enter any common room in Oxford between the hours
of six and nine in the evening, you would have been
safe to hear some ten or twenty voices eloquent on the
subject of Tract XC. If you had happened to pass two
heads of houses, or tutors of Colleges, strolling down
High Street in the afternoon, or returning from their
walk over Magdalen Bridge, a thousand to one but you
would have caught the words 'Newman' and
'Tract XC.'" Newman, although unprepared for the

reception his pamphlet received, says that he felt no fear, but, in one point of view, a sense of relief. He saw plainly that confidence was at an end, and that his place in the movement was gone. In fact, he was regarded as a traitor, as one who would betray the citadel he was sworn to defend. He was urged to withdraw the Tract, but refused. An "understanding" was entered into that it should not be condemned, on condition that he did not defend it, that he stopped the series, and that he himself published his own condemnation in a letter to the Bishop of Oxford. "I agreed," says Newman; "no written pledge was given. It was an 'understanding.' I have hated them ever since." The cry was up, and the opponents of the movement were determined to strike. Four of the leading tutors—Mr. Tait, the present Archbishop of Canterbury, was one of them, and Mr. H. B. Wilson, subsequently a contributor to *Essays and Reviews,* was another—wrote a letter stating that the Tract had a tendency to mitigate the differences between Roman and Anglican doctrine. The Hebdomadal Council, consisting of Heads of Houses and other influential officers of the University, met to consider the complaint of the four tutors. Newman had explained in a letter to Dr. Jelf, and had a fuller explanation in the press, stating that he considered that " the Thirty-nine Articles *do* contain a condemnation of the authoritative teaching of the Church of Rome upon the very subjects upon which the four tutors had alleged that he suggested that they do *not.*" In this letter he uncon-

D

sciously sounded a note of alarm by stating that he had been urged to write the Tract by persons he revered, "to keep members of our own Church from straggling in the direction of Rome." This was an indication of the real danger that underlay the Tractarian movement. Still the measure of alarm was no warrant for the impetuosity of action which followed. The Hebdomadal Board were asked for a respite of twelve hours, but refused to grant it, although they knew that by condemning Newman they were condemning Keble, if not Pusey as well, to whom the offending volume had been submitted, and by the former of whom its publication was sanctioned. It was resolved that "the modes of interpretation such as are suggested in the same Tract, evading rather than explaining the sense of the Thirty-nine Articles, and reconciling subscription to them with the adoption of errors which they were designed to counteract, defeat the object, and are inconsistent with the due observations, of the above-mentioned statutes,"— meaning the statutes which require every student to be instructed in, and subscribe to the Thirty-nine Articles.

Hitherto, the authorship of the Tract had been only suspected, not avowed. Now, however, Newman, determined that those who had condemned it should gain nothing by pleading vagueness of application, came forward and acknowledged formally what everyone had already taken for granted. He made this acknowledgment in a letter of touching humility, addressed to the Vice-Chancellor. It ran as follows :—

, " Mr. Vice-Chancellor,

" I write this respectfully to inform you that I am the author, and have the sole responsibility of the Tract on which the Hebdomadal Board has just now expressed an opinion, and that I have not given my name hitherto, under the belief that it was desired that I should not. I hope it will not surprise you if I say that my opinion remains unchanged of the truth and honesty of the principle maintained in the Tract, and of the necessity of putting it forth. At the same time, I am prompted by my feelings to add my deep consciousness that everything I attempt might be done in a better spirit, and in a better way ; and, while I am sincerely sorry for the trouble and anxiety I have given to the members of the Board, I beg to return my thanks to them for an act which, even though founded on misapprehension, may be made as profitable to myself as it is religiously and charitably intended. I say all this with great sincerity,

"And am, Mr. Vice-Chancellor,

" Your obedient servant,

" JOHN HENRY NEWMAN."

The precipitancy of the Hebdomadal Council has been much condemned. Mr. Justice Coleridge, in his *Life of Keble*, says, "The Council was substantially a Court before which their indictment" (the letter of the four tutors) "was brought for trial. We all know to what any person accused before any judge is entitled. Here, when the letter and the Tract were laid before the Council, it had both the charge and the evidence offered in support of it. It may be taken that it was not a usual course in such a case to summon the party, or even to give him any notice of what was impending, and, therefore, however strange such a practice may be, it cannot fairly be said that any special unfairness is to be complained of for the want of this. But the Council knew and were, indeed, directly informed that three individuals, among the most eminent in the University and most blameless in character, were substantially the persons to be affected by their decree; nor could the Council be ignorant how heavy was the blow which it was proposed to strike by its sentence. The barest justice, therefore, required that if any one of them desired to be heard in explanation or mitigation of the charge, reasonable time should have been afforded for the purpose; the more plain the case, the stronger seemingly the evidence, the more imperative in a judicial proceeding was this duty. One can hardly believe that five days only elapsed from the commencement of the proceeding to the publication of the sentence; and twelve hours were respectfully solicited and refused; on the sixth day the defence appeared." There is too much reason to believe that the eagerness of the judges to condemn was due to their strong feeling against the movement. Impartiality could scarcely have been looked for in such a case. Yet the act they were determined on was one of momentous importance and far-reaching consequences. "No one can tell how much of the subsequent history of the Church of England might not have been altered had that respite of twelve hours been granted." It was contended that the Council was not an authoritative representation of the University, and therefore that its condemnation had no binding effect; as a matter of fact Newman had been condemned by no legally constituted Court, and no existing law had been broken; but any hopes that might have been built upon this view were dispelled by the strongly-expressed desire of the Bishop of the Diocese that the Tracts should be discontinued. The voice of authority could not be disputed by those who were themselves the great champions of authority. In a letter to the Bishop of Oxford, Newman touchingly resigned his place in the movement: "I have nothing to be sorry for," he said, "except having made your Lordship anxious, and others whom I am bound to revere. I have nothing to be sorry for, but everything to rejoice in and be thankful for. I have never taken pleasure in seeming to be able to move a party, and whatever influence I have had has been found, not sought after. I have acted because others did not act, and have sacrificed a quiet which I prized. May God be with me in time to come, as He has been hitherto; and He will be, if I can but keep my hand clean and my heart pure. I think I can bear, or at least will try to bear, any personal humiliation, so that I am preserved from betraying sacred interests, which the Lord of grace and power has given into my charge."

Three or four years later a proposal was made in the Academical Convocation to formally condemn Tract XC, but it was stopped by the veto of the two Proctors. At the time of its publication, pamphlets were written on both sides, and the strife continued with exceeding bitterness. Most people condemned the Tract as evasive, and charged its author with intellectual dishonesty. The Tractarians, as Newman himself admits, had at length come into collision with the nation. Whatever the historical argument in their favour, the principles of the Protestant Reformation had been rudely assailed. The feeling of hostility to them was all the greater because the growth of the *Via Media* was occasioning considerable alarm. Its advocates preached to crowded churches. A Bishop in his charge said, " It is daily assuming a more serious and alarming aspect. Under the specious pretence of deference to antiquity and respect for primitive models, the foundations of the Protestant Church are undermined by men who dwell within her walls, and those who sit in the Reformer's seat are traducing the Reformation."

The next chapter will show the consequences to which the movement led ; but it may be noted here that during all this critical time Mr. Newman's literary activity was considerable. From 1838 to 1843 he was editor of the *British Critic,* a periodical which had a considerable influence in shaping the movement of which he was the head. He contributed several articles to its pages, and gathered round him a staff of able writers. These articles, we are told by one of his contemporaries, were looked out for with anxiety, recognised with ease, and read with eagerness. " I believe I am correct," says Canon Oakeley, " in saying that it was Mr. Newman's articles in the *Critic* which led to his being invited by the proprietors of the *Times* to come out in that journal with some remarks upon literary projects of the day, and that the result of these overtures may be seen in the celebrated letters of ' Catholicus.' " These letters made such an impression upon the directors of the *Times* that they were anxious to obtain Newman's services regularly on their staff. He was offered a large salary, one report says as much as £1,800 a year. "Shall I be free," asked the young man to whom this tempting offer was made, "to say what I think?" The reply may be imagined, and Newman declined the proposal. "How different," says a commentator on this circumstance, "might have been the course of recent English history if Newman had yielded to the temptation, or the *Times* had promised him the liberty 'to say what he thought'!"

CHAPTER III.

PROGRESS OF THE "VIA MEDIA"—NEWMAN'S RETRACTATION—RESIGNS LIVING OF ST. MARY'S—LITTLEMORE MONASTERY—THE ECCLESIASTICAL MIRACLES—A MEMORABLE YEAR—VISIT OF FATHER DOMINIC—FORMAL SECESSION TO ROME—MR. OAKELEY'S ACCOUNT—SENSATION CAUSED BY THE EVENT—OTHER SECESSIONS—FALSE RUMOURS—NEWMAN QUITS OXFORD—THE INTELLECTUAL RECOVERY OF ROMANISM.

THE *Via Media*, as its name imports, was to be a "middle way" between the Church of England and the Church of Rome; but it proved, to a good many of those who journeyed by it, the direct path to Rome itself. Of the "perverts," as they were called, none

equalled either in intellect or influence, the subject of
this sketch. His secession, although it cannot be said
to have been unlooked for, caused a great shock
throughout the Protestant world. It was felt that
whatever might be the extent of the loss to the
Reformed Church, the gain to Rome was enormous.
For some time before the irrevocable step was taken
there had been a growing expectation that there could
be but one climax to the processes of development
which were going on in Newman's mind, and that the
drama of which he was the central and dominant
figure could have but one *dénouement*. But the stages,
if we may judge from his own narrative, were not so
well defined to him as they were to lookers on, nor did
the end seem so certain. But from the crisis of the
Tractarian movement the progress which he made
Romewards was steady and unbroken. " From the end
of 1841," he says, " I was on my death-bed as regards
my membership with the Anglican Church, though at
the time I became aware of it only by degrees." The
various causes which contributed to this great and
significant departure have been set forth by himself
with so much minuteness and candour that it would be
superfluous to indicate them here. The great point, of
course, had reference to the rival claims of the two
Churches to Authority A desire to invest the Anglican
Church with a richer ceremonial, and to introduce into
her rites some,—such as prayers for the dead, and
reverence for the Virgin Mary,—which had hitherto
been considered Romish, if not distinctively Roman,

was but a minor phase of the metamorphosis that was taking place. Newman was a long while, comparatively speaking, in making up his mind. He had ceased to be in full sympathy with the Anglican Communion some time before he sought admission to that of Rome. Nor is it possible to condemn the precision with which he acted, after reading his own account of the event, and of the hesitations, doubts, difficulties, and struggles which oppressed him as each new argument presented itself. The censures passed upon him at the time, for retaining his benefice in the Church of England after he had been troubled with grave misgivings about her right to be considered the true and Apostolic Church, fail very much of their effect in the light of his own frank narrative. He determined, he tells us, to be guided, not by his imagination, but by his reason; otherwise he would have been, he says, a Catholic sooner than he was. The world saw, more promptly than he did, whither he was drifting. Those who were observing him understood him better than he understood himself. It was Newman's honest belief at the time that "the deep chasm across the path," to which reference has already been made, had an actual existence; but his views progressed by "leaps and bounds," and every month made the prediction of those who could see nothing but Rome as the upshot of it all, appear more likely of fulfilment, and the chances very strong of the chasm vanishing altogether Step by step he got nearer to the goal. Men instinctively felt what was coming when, in 1843, he made a formal retractation of all the hard things he had said against the Church of Rome, and followed it, six or seven months later, by resigning the living of St. Mary's.

The humility of the former of these steps has scarcely ever been equalled in modern times. He had some hard things to unsay. In 1833, in the *Lyra Apostolica* he had called Rome " a lost Church." In his work on the Arians he had spoken of "the Papal Apostacy." In the fifteenth of the *Tracts for the Times* he said of Rome that she was " heretic," that she had " apostatized in the Council of Trent," and that she had "joined herself in perpetual league to the cause of Antichrist." In the twentieth Tract he wrote that the Roman Communion was " infected with heresy, and ought to be shunned like the Plague." In 1834, he spoke of " the corrupt system of the Papacy," and of the Roman Church as " invaded by an evil genius." And in the thirty-eighth Tract he applied to the doctrines of the Roman Church, the epithets " anti-scriptural, profane, impious, audacious, without authority, gross, monstrous, and cruel." Having cited these condemnations, and formally retracted them, he said, " If you ask me how an individual could have dared, not only to conceive, but even to publish such opinions upon a Communion so ancient, so widely extended—a Communion which has produced so many saints—I give you in answer what I said to myself: ' I am not speaking my own words ; I am but following almost a consensus of the divines of my Church. They have ever used the strongest language against Rome, even the most able

and learned of them. I wish to throw myself into
their system. While I say what they say, I am safe.
Such views, too, are necessary for our position. Yet
I have reason to fear still, that such language is to be
ascribed in no small measure to an impetuous temper,
a hope of approving myself to persons I respect, and a
wish to repel the charge of Romanism."

The resignation of the living of St. Mary's, it was
manifest, was the beginning of the end. We can
readily imagine what a pang it must have been to Dr.
Newman to cut himself adrift from associations and
friendships so close and tender as those which were
identified with the Protestant period of his life. The
magnitude of the sacrifice he made is the strongest
proof of the complete sincerity of his proceeding. In
the Church of England he might reasonably have
looked forward, despite the antagonism aroused by the
teaching put forward in Tract XC, to the natural
reward of his high character, conspicuous piety, and
unrivalled talents. No position would have been too
lofty for his reasonable aspirations, had he been one of
those who hungered after the flesh-pots of Egypt. But
by his resignation of St. Mary's he virtually gave it
forth that the Anglican Church was no longer a home
or a resting-place for him. The admission must have
been, in many ways, a great shock to his feelings.
Very intimate relationships were severed; very tender
memories were torn up by the roots. In the remarkable
semi-controversial story, *Loss and Gain; or the Story of
a Convert*, published some three years after his formal

secession, he has set forth, with great power of pathos
the piercing anguish which a step of this kind causes
where family convictions and prejudices are at work.
The hero of the story, Charles Reding, cannot, of course,
be accepted as a counterpart of Dr. Newman himself;
but, no doubt, his own feelings entered largely into the
composition of the character, and the experience of his
own mind, in those moments of turmoil and uncertainty, may be supposed to have coloured the fictional
portrait of the typical "pervert" who, moved by a
high and conscientious conviction, cut himself adrift
from ties of the dearest and most intimate kind, and
wounded the friends whom he most fondly loved.
Newman must have felt acutely the "loss" of the
step he was about taking; not the material "loss"—he
was far too spiritually-minded for anything of that kind
—but the loss of old friends, and the tearing asunder
of old associations. St. Mary's had been the scene of
his great triumphs as a preacher. It was there that
the subtle eloquence of his sermons had been lavished
on rapt and eager hearers. It cannot have been
with a light heart that he resigned his living, and
retired to the comparative seclusion of Littlemore,
where he had recently established an ascetic community on a mediæval model.

Over this community, which was in purpose an
Anglican retreat, he presided for three years. Littlemore was a favourite spot with him. "For several
years," says Mr. Oakeley, "he had spent in its
grateful seclusion the penitential seasons of the Church,

and probably had long looked to it as one day to be the scene of a still more complete retirement, and a still more ascetic mode of life. Rumour soon became busy as to the probability of his carrying some such plan into effect; and the dons, who at this time were apt to take their afternoon stroll in the direction of Littlemore, remarked, in significant phrase, that what used to be a mere cluster of cottages was assuming, under the hands of carpenters and masons, a somewhat monastic appearance. It was not long before these suspicions were fully confirmed. Mr. Newman's visits to Littlemore became less frequent only because they were of longer duration; and somewhere, I think, about the end of the year 1842 he took up his abode, with several young men who had attached themselves to his person and his fortunes, in the building which was not long in vindicating to itself the name of Littlemore Monastery. Up to the summer of 1843, Mr. Newman continued to officiate in the church which had been erected in the forementioned village under his skilful eye. But somewhere about that period, as well as I can remember, he took his final leave of the Protestant pulpit in a sermon of singular beauty and memorable interest to all his friends, who wept audibly, as they felt only too surely convinced that the voice so familiar to them was to be hushed." Littlemore was endeared to him, as much by the struggles and perturbations of a questioning and unsettled time, as by the recollection of the calmer period which had prefaced the spiritual tempest in which he had been so troubled and tossed. Yet the associations of the village were, by and bye, to be disturbed like those of the city. The conviction had slowly forced itself upon his mind that he had been on the wrong road. His dream of a *Via Media* had long been consigned to the limbo of unrealisable ideals,—to the lumber-room of impracticable hopes. Arguments which were satisfactory to his own mind, and which never faltered in their force in his after life, conveyed to him the conviction that the Church of Rome was the only true Christian Church, that its bishops were in direct apostolical succession, that its antiquity was indisputable, and that it exercised the only legitimate authority among the competing claimants of Christendom. We are not called upon to test those arguments now. A man's adoption of a new faith is a matter for his own conscience alone. The sneer of "perversion" is at all times an unworthy one. Moreover, it is a two-edged sword that may chance to cut those who wield it as well as those at whom it is aimed. In Newman's case, at all events, there was no fair ground for the hard words with which, prior to his secession as well as after it, his change of opinions was received. We may regret that change—we may deplore the effect of the reasoning he adopted,—but we cannot deny him all the credit due to conscientiousness and honesty Having persuaded himself that the Church of Rome was the true one, he exhibited the courage of his convictions, and "went over." Others, whose doctrinal differences were not easily distinguishable from his own, remained within the Anglican fold. From that day to this there have been priests who have received the emoluments and eaten the bread of the Church of England, while persistently enunciating principles antagonistic to the spirit of the Reformation. Secession has, at least, the merit of straightforwardness and consistency over such a course as theirs; and if Dr. Newman's conclusions seemed ever so wrong, Protestants could not with any grace condemn him for accepting the full consequences of those conclusions.

By this time the mystical element of his nature had become firmly allied to what many people, not necessarily lacking in devoutness, would call superstition. The phase of his mind which was conspicuous in childhood—a strong belief in the magical and supernatural—had grown with his growth, and strengthened with his strength. He enunciated views on the Ecclesiastical Miracles which shocked men of sober sense. He accepted stories so apparently impossible that harsh critics felt inclined to pronounce the vigorous intellect in its dotage. All the fables of mediæval lore were received with a scarcely questioning faith He believed in all the fanciful legends clustering round the story of St. Ambrose; he believed in the fable of the Thundering Legion; he believed in the change of water into oil by St. Narcissus, of Jerusalem, to supply the lamps on the vigil of Easter; he believed in the miracle reputed to have been wrought on the course of the river Lycus by Gregory Thaumaturgus; he believed in the discovery of the Holy Cross; he believed in the miraculous recovery of their speech by the sixty African confessors after their tongues had been cut out to the roots by order of Hunneric. He believed all this, and avowed his belief, and justified himself by means of arguments which to more sceptical men than himself looked like a tissue of elaborate sophistries. In short, he threw himself, without any reserve, into the whole mediæval system of religion in the Latin Church. A series of *Lives of the Saints,* of which he was the editor sanctioned shocks of a similar kind, and repeated in the gravest manner incidents that might have passed muster in a fairy tale, but were too wonderful to have found a place in what purported to be a sober record of fact. Yet no one can question that Newman believed most implicitly in all these things himself. The structure of his mind not only enabled, but encouraged him to do so. Even while we may feel convinced that he is being misled by his own subtlety, it is impossible for us not to admire his transparent sincerity.

All this was leading on to Rome. It was in 1845, two years after his resignation of St. Mary's, that he took the last and most important step. This was in many ways an eventful year in the history of the Church. In February, Ward's *Ideal of a Christian Church* had been condemned in the Oxford Convocation, and the author had been deprived of his degrees, notwithstanding the support of some influential men, amongst whom was Mr. Gladstone. In April, the

country was greatly excited about Sir Robert Peel's
proposal to grant £30,000 a year to Maynooth College.
In June, Sir Jenner Fust condemned Mr. Oakeley for
claiming to hold the same tenets as Mr. Ward. Then,
in October, came Newman's secession. Previous to it
he had been hard at his *Essay on Doctrinal Development.*
"As I advanced," he says, "my view so cleared that
instead of speaking any more of 'the Roman Catholics,'
I boldly called them Catholics. Before I got to the end
I resolved to be received, and the book remains in the
state in which it was then, unfinished." The object of
this work was to show that the obstacles which he had
formerly written of as existing to communion with the
Church of Rome had, in his developed judgment, no
real foundation. The letter in which he announced to
his more particular friends the resolution at which he
had arrived, deserves a place in this record :—

"Littlemore, October 8, 1845.

"I am this night expecting Father Dominic, the Passionist,
who, from his youth, has been led to have distinct and direct
thoughts, first of the countries of the North, then of England.
After thirty years' (almost) waiting, he was without his own act
sent here. But he has had little to do with conversions. I saw
him here for a few minutes on St. John Baptist's Day last year.
He does not know of my intention; but I mean to ask of him
admission into the one Fold of Christ. . . . I have so many
letters to write, that this must do for all who choose to ask about
me. . . . P.S.—This will not go till all is over. Of course,
it requires no answer."

Father Dominic was summoned in hot haste from
Aston Hall to Littlemore, "to fulfil a work in God's
service." He did not know what was wanted of him,

E

but started at once and without delay, and notwithstanding the rain, which fell in torrents, arrived after a
journey of five hours, dripping wet, at Littlemore.   On
his admission to the house, Newman flung himself
humbly at his feet, saying that he would not rise until
the Father had blessed him and received him "into the
Church of Jesus Christ."   "The Father," says Don
James Margotti, the editor of the *Unità Cattolica*, "was
at once conscious of a great miracle of grace, and,
moved to tears, he received the neophyte with the most
loving welcome ; and, having spent all the night with
him in prayer, on the morrow (October 10th) he
accepted his abjuration, and reconciled him with the
mother Church, baptising him under solemn conditions,
and comforting him with the Holy Eucharist."

The historical character of this memorable event
must be pleaded as an excuse for once more quoting
from the pages of Mr. Oakeley.   "It was a memorable
day, that 9th of October, 1845.   The rain came down in
torrents, bringing with it the first heavy instalment of
autumn's sere and yellow leaves.   The wind, like a
spent giant, howled forth the expiring notes of its
equinoctial fury   The superstitious might have said
that the very elements were on the side of Anglicanism
—so copiously did they weep, so piteously bemoan, the
approaching departure of its great representative.   The
bell, which swung visibly in the turret of the little
gothic church at Littlemore, gave that day the usual
notice of morning and afternoon prayers ; but it came
to the ear in that buoyant, bouncing tone which is usual

in a high wind, and sounded like a knell rather than a summons. The monastery was more than usually sombre and still. Egress and ingress there were none that day; for it had been given out, among friends accustomed to visit there, that Mr. Newman 'wished to remain quiet.' One of these friends, who resided in the neighbourhood, had been used to attend the evening 'office' in the oratory of the house, but he was forbidden to come 'for two or three days, for reasons which would be explained later.' The 9th of the month passed off without producing any satisfaction to the general curiosity. All that transpired was that a remarkable-looking man, evidently a foreigner, and shabbily dressed in black, had asked his way to Mr. Newman's on the day but one before; and the rumour was that he was a Catholic priest. In the course of a day or two the friend before mentioned was re-admitted to the evening office, and found that a change had come over it. The Latin was pronounced for the first time in the Roman way, and the antiphons of Our Lady, which up to that day had always been omitted, came out in their proper place. The friend in question would have asked the reason of these changes, but it was forbidden to speak to any of the community after night-prayers. Very soon the mystery was cleared up by Mr. Newman and his companions appearing at mass in the public chapel at Oxford."

It would be difficult, perhaps, to exaggerate the sensation which this step made in the religious world, and even beyond its borders. In some quarters it was received with anger, and "that traitor Newman" was held up to much vehemence of abuse. He has himself described somewhere the penalties which are visited on "the Papal pervert," and in his own experience he underwent them to the letter. Men did not then thoroughly understand him. They fancied there was something moving behind the scenes,—that there were undercurrents of motive below the ostensible reasons assigned. Many years elapsed before Dr. Newman's own countrymen were convinced of the mistake they had made. For a time the air was filled with the echoes of their railing. It is questionable, however, if even those who were loudest in their condemnation fully appreciated the magnitude of the conquest which Rome had made. We of a later age have been able to recognise the full importance of her gain, and its significant bearing on the current religious movements of the second half of the nineteenth century. Mr. Gladstone, indeed, writing many years after, remarked: "In my opinion his (Dr. Newman's) secession from the Church of England has never yet been estimated among us at anything like the full amount of its calamitous importance. It has been said that the world does not know its greatest men ; neither, I will add, is it aware of the power and weight carried by the words and the acts of those among its greatest men whom it does know The ecclesiastical historian will perhaps hereafter judge that this secession was a much greater event even than the partial secession of John Wesley, the only case of personal loss suffered by the Church of England since the Reformation, which can be at all compared with it in magnitude. I do not refer to its effect upon the mere balance of schools or parties in the Church; that is an inferior question. I refer to its effect upon the state of positive belief, and the attitude and capacities of the religious mind of England."

There can be very little question that Dr. Newman's secession had a considerable tendency to unsettle men's beliefs. So commanding an intellect, it was argued, would never have rendered allegiance to Rome except on the strength of historical facts which were at least deserving of respectful consideration. Many who had not hitherto questioned the validity of the Protestant position experienced, for the first time in their lives, a vague and painful uncertainty. Here, they said, was a man of profound erudition and earnest piety, who had thrown up everything, under the overwhelming conviction that the Church of England was historically a delusion and the Reformation a great wrong. Such an act was sufficient to cause a widespread disorganisation. Those, perhaps, who had the gravest right of protest were the members of that school which the Tractarian party had been at such pains to form within the Church. They had been led forth and left to their own devices. Many of them shrank from the conclusions of their quondam leader, but their position was none the more enviable on that account. He who had once declared Rome to be Anti-Christ had now thrown in his lot with Rome. A band of sympathisers followed, or immediately preceded him—Hope Scott, Frederick

Faber, Ward of the *Ideal*, the two Wilberforces, and a few others They were faithful friends, and zealous men enough, and some of them were characterized by ability, but they were not persons of any great mark. Newman himself loomed so large upon the popular imagination that there was no room on the disc for mere secondary personages. Those who expected a great movement of secession, like that of the Free Kirk, were mistaken. Still, the number who followed the great Tractarian was sufficiently large to produce a profound sensation. Never had so large a body of the English clergy seceded since the Reformation. The Protestants under Edward the Sixth, imitating the tactics of the Vicar of Bray, became Catholics under Mary, and Protestants again under Elizabeth. Under Laud, too, a movement was progressing in the direction of Popery, which was only prevented from attaining its full development by the greater urgency and importance of his political schemes. But as a genuine change of faith, unaffected by personal interests, there had been nothing like the Tractarian secession since the Church had become Protestant. Disraeli testifies that the Anglican Church reeled under the shock of Dr. Newman's withdrawal, and the heart of the nation was just as profoundly moved. The occasion led to much bitter misrepresentation. The group of "perverts" were subjected to all the rash and reckless spirit of slander which prevailed at the time. Dr. Newman himself was the chief mark of this malicious misrepresentation. It was rumoured

that he was mad; it was rumoured that he had
quarrelled with the authorities at Rome and had been
suspended; it was even rumoured that he had given up
Christianity altogether, and had fallen back upon some
scheme of natural religion foreign alike to his training
and his instincts. It is needless to say that all these
rumours were false. The change of opinion which so
greatly excited his adversaries at any rate brought
peace to him. He has himself told us that his admission into the Communion of Rome was like getting
into harbour after being tossed about on a stormy sea.
Under such circumstances the persistent and bitter
attacks of the religious papers must have been deprived
of the worst effects of their sting, and the rash prophecies
of the critics must have been lightened of their annoy-
ance by the humour of their absurdity. A great deal
was written and said about his " perversion." Sermons
were preached about him, pamphlets were written,
lectures were delivered, he was fulminated against in
good round terms by every sound Protestant. Even the
wits found material for their fancy in the course he
had taken. By and bye, opinion cooled down. People
gave up trying to understand what was evidently beyond
their intellectual depth. Lord John Russell summarised
the popular judgment when he ventured upon the astute
observation that Dr. Newman's secession was "an
inexplicable event." It was not for some years that a
light was thrown upon the incident, which gave it a
rational and intelligible character. That light, as will be
presently shown, was thrown by Dr. Newman himself.

It remains but to say in connection with this part of the narrative that Dr. Newman quitted Oxford finally on February 23rd, 1846. He had in the meantime received the official congratulations of Dr. Wiseman, and in reply thereto had expressed a wish to minister "in a humble way" in the Catholic Church. His leave-taking with the University was full of a pathos which only those can appreciate who have voluntarily and from a high sense of duty severed themselves from old and dear associations. "Trinity," he says, speaking of his first College, "had never been unkind to me. There used to be much snapdragon growing on the walls opposite my freshman's rooms there, and I had for years taken it as the emblem of my own perpetual residence even unto death in my University." During the next three and thirty years, Dr. Newman never saw Oxford "excepting its spires, as they are seen from the railway."

The effects of this memorable change of creed can scarcely be properly estimated, even now. There was not, as has been already said, a great secession at the time, but the effects of it are not spent even yet. Dr. Newman set the tide rolling in the direction of Romanism. He approved it with the seal of his genius, and many a weaker man, putting trust in his superior gifts, has made Newman's withdrawal the apology for his own. Mr. J. A. Froude sums up the consequences of his conduct in the following passage :— "To him, if to any one man, the world owes the intellectual recovery of Romanism. Fifty years ago it was in England a dying creed, lingering in retirement in the halls and chapels of a few half-forgotten families. A shy Oxford student has come out on its behalf into the field of controversy, armed with the keenest weapons of modern learning and philosophy; and wins illustrious converts, and has kindled hopes that England herself, the England of Elizabeth and Cromwell, will kneel for absolution again before the Father of Christendom. Mr. Buckle questioned whether any great work has ever been done in this world by an individual man. Newman, by the solitary force of his own mind, has produced this extraordinary change. What he has done we all see; what will come of it our children will see. Of the magnitude of the phenomenon itself no reasonable person can doubt. Two writers have affected powerfully the present generation of Englishmen. Newman is one, Thomas Carlyle is the other. But Carlyle has been at issue with all the tendencies of his age. Like a John the Baptist, he has stood alone, preaching repentance in a world which is to him a wilderness; Newman has been the voice of the intellectual reaction of Europe, which was alarmed by an era of revolutions, and is looking for safety in the forsaken beliefs of the ages which it has been tempted to despise."

CHAPTER IV.

Oscott—"Herr Newman's Pilgrimage"—Visits Rome—Founda-
tion of the Birmingham Oratory—St. Philip Neri—
Newman's Admiration of the Saint—The Alcester Street
Mission—The Cholera Epidemic at Bilston—Removal
of the Oratory to Edgbaston—The Irish Catholic
University.

"Dr. Wiseman, in whose vicariate Oxford lay, called
me to Oscott; and I went there with others; afterwards
he sent me to Rome, and finally placed me in Birmingham." Thus Dr. Newman himself briefly chronicles
his early movements in his new sphere. On the feast
of All Saints, November 1st, he received, together with
Mr. Oakeley and his Littlemore companions, the gift of
"the Holy Ghost in the Sacrament of Confirmation," at
St. Mary's, Oscott, by the Right Rev. Dr. Wiseman himself, and soon after he set forth on his continental
journey. This "pilgrimage," as it was called, furnished
some material for the scoffers. Dr. Newman's faith in
miracles, and his ready acceptance of the supernatural,
provoked ridicule in certain quarters. It is, perhaps,
hardly worth while to disinter from the forgotten pages
of a periodical the fugitive *jeux d'ésprit* of the day, but
one which appeared under the title of "Herr Newman's
Pilgrimage," in the *Dublin University Magazine*, is a
sufficiently fair sample of the rest, and a few lines of it

may be quoted, more for the purpose of showing the spirit of the times than because the rhymes deserve to be remembered.

* * * * * *

"Newman, saintly, sad, and sage,
Takes the staff of pilgrimage,
A tooth of St. Denis is in his scrip—
A silver tooth with a socket of gold,
And a hair from the mole on St. Katherine's lip,
Which blotted her face like an iron-mould."

* * * * * *

"Forth upon his pilgrimage
Moves the man of middle age,—
Ever as he went he told
One by one his beads of gold;
Angel voices meet his ear,
Waking thoughts of happy cheer—
Visions of an elder day,
And old rhymes made short his way,
And thus he said, or seemed to say,
'How happily Tertullian,
How sweetly, too, St. Cyprian—
Like our dear young Faber, paints
The lilies of the Church—her saints!'
'Oh happy days'—thus runs their praise—
'When children seven each virgin had—
The first a boy in white was clad,
Modesty, a fair-haired boy;
And the second's name was Joy;
Patience next with sober glance,
Meekness, Prudence, Temperance;
And last and loveliest of the seven,
Chastity, with heart in heaven.'

In such scales of silver weighing,
By such test their gold assaying,
And a sigh of pity heaving
For poor England unbelieving,
Virgin thousands, ten and one,
He hath honoured at Cologne.

Heads of St. Cornelius three,
('Twenty-four in all there be),
Now he makes belief to see.

One had eyes, whence lightnings broke,
One the Flemish language spoke,
One a Turkish pipe did smoke.

With a jewelled turban one
Like a sheik of Babylon
Was apparelled; one had on
An Oxford cap—and one a crown.

As our pilgrim bowed his head,
Enemies in whispers said,
That in adoration dread
He was worshipping the Dead.

Dead men's heads these never were:
One is huckabuck and hair—
One is parchment puffed with air—
One is China's earthenware.

One of them with white lips mute
Moved his eyes in stern salute;
Like a statue frozen-eyed,
One with hollow words replied.

And the third grave head did shake;
And a stirring light 'gan wake,
As it were a living soul,
In that Eastern meerschaum's bowl

Is it but the necromancy
Of our pilgrim's burning fancy?
Or are phantom's rising slow
From the dark abysses low,
Whither the dead attorneys go,
And the living shall also?

Strange it is to see the springs
Of his spirit with the strings,
Stirring, that command the eyes
Of that Mandarin to rise.

On a scaffold to adore,
Twelve feet raised from the church floor,
He was kneeling. Does the light
Disturb his vision ?—is the height
Too high to which his raptures rise ?

On seraph's wings he soars, he flies.
Higher and higher still he rose,
In his own dream, till—down he goes.

Was the scaffolding broken on which he relied ?
Has his fall, after all, but been caused by his pride ?
I know not—I guess not—I tell but the last,
That NEWMAN HAS FALL'N, AND IS PROBABLY CRACKED."

He reached Rome on the 28th October, 1846, in the early months of Pius the IXth's pontificate. The next day he hastened to pray at the Confession of St. Peter, and the fervour of his supplications attracted the attention of Pio Nono, who, by a singular coincidence, advanced at the same moment. The Pontiff knew nothing of Newman; he was, however, moved by his unusual devotions. Nevertheless, for a recent convert of the stamp of Newman, such an event could not be without significance. We have it on the authority of Alfonso Capecelatro, the priest of the Oratory of Naples, that so unwilling was Dr. Newman, to receive an exalted position, that on his arrival at Rome he wished to enter the College of the Propaganda as a simple student.

On his return to England he was directed to establish in Birmingham the Oratory, which has since achieved, in a large measure through the eminence of its founder, a world-wide distinction It was dedicated to St. Philip Neri, the founder of the congregation of the Oratory of Italy, whose pious and devoted life and " bright and beautiful character" had won Dr. Newman's love and devotion even when he was a Protestant. The golden legends of the hagiology may contain records of more heroic sacrifice and tales of more enduring suffering, but it is doubtful if they contain the story of a purer or more perfectly religious life. If it lacked the fanatical self-mortifications of a Stylites, it was full of earnest well-doing and saintly zeal. St. Philip was born in 1515, at Florence, and by his blameless conduct early gained for himself the name of "Good Philip." Intended by his father for a commercial life, he soon showed a predilection for the service of religion, and won esteem both for his great learning and his self-denying piety. He went to Rome, formed a congregation or society with the object of reclaiming the worldly, gained repute as a preacher, visited the hospitals, held theological conferences, and spent a life of singular devotion and simplicity. His last days on earth have been touchingly described by Bacci. He lived to a ripe old age, dying in 1595, at Rome, after receiving the Viaticum from the hands of Cardinal Frederick Borromeo; and was canonized by Gregory XV. in 1622. Dr. Newman entertained for the memory of this "old man of sweet aspect" a strong personal attachment, and his benign and exemplary influence are traceable throughout the Oratory. The modern institution was, indeed, an attempt to reproduce a chapter of the sixteenth century, and to realize a more or less ideal picture of corporate saintliness.

Dr. Newman, like the prototype for whose sweet and perfect life he had such reverence, was for many years simply a priest without ecclesiastical rank or titular distinction ; like him, too, he was a man of deep learning and of unselfish zeal. There was, indeed, much in common between the two men, and the sentiment and spirit of St. Philip's work have been applied to modern conditions with no mean success by the eminent man whom the Roman Church was so fortunate as to capture. All his life has been affected by the subtle influence of his saintly exemplar. What in other hands would have been a fantastic attempt to reproduce the past, became in his a revitalising of the present by aid of the example of the illustrious piety of three hundred years ago. Dr. Newman has made frequent allusion to the Saint in his writings,— especially in his poems. He has pictured him in his Mission, in himself, in his God, in his School, and in his Disciples. In one of these poems he says—

" Yet there is one I more affect
    Than Jesuit, Hermit, Monk, or Friar,
'Tis an old man of sweet aspèct,
    I love him more, I more admire.

I know him by his head of snow,
    His ready smile, his keen full eye,
His words which kindle as they flow,
    Save he be rapt in ecstasy."

And, writing of " St. Philip in his Mission," he makes a beautiful reference to the spirit of the work in which he and his colleagues were engaged :—

" In the far North our lot is cast,
  Where faithful hearts are few ;
Still are we Philip's children dear,
  And Peter's soldiers true.

Founder and Sire ! to mighty Rome,
  Beneath St. Peter's shade,
Early thy vow of loyal love
  And ministry was paid.

          *   *   *   *

And first in the old catacombs,
  In galleries long and deep,
Where martyr Popes had ruled the flock,
  And slept their glorious sleep,

There didst thou pass the nights in pray'r
  Until at length there came,
Down on thy breast, new lit for thee,
  The Pentecostal flame ;—

Then, in that heart-consuming love,
  Didst walk the city wide,
And lure the noble and the young
  From Babel's pomp and pride ;

And gathering them within thy cell,
  Unveil the lustre bright,
And beauty of thy inner soul,
  And gain them by the sight.

          *   *   *   *

And as the Apostle, on the hill
  Facing the Imperial Town,
First gazed upon his fair domain,
  Then on the cross lay down ;

So thou, from out the streets of Rome
  Didst turn thy failing eye
Unto that mount of martyrdom,
  Take leave of it, and die."

In his *Idea of a University*, Dr. Newman has dwelt
with eloquence on the character of his "own Father

and Patron." "He came to the Eternal City"—to quote one passage,—"and he sat himself down there, and his home and his family grew up around him, by the spontaneous accession of materials from without. He did not so much seek his own as draw them to him. He sat in his small room, and they in their gay worldly dresses, the rich and the well-born, as well as the simple and the illiterate, crowded into it. In the mid-heats of summer, in the frosts of winter, still was he in that low and narrow cell at San Girolamo, reading the hearts of those who came to him, and curing · their souls' maladies by the very touch of his hand. And they who came remained gazing and listening, till at length, first one and then another threw off their bravery, and took his poor cassock and girdle instead; or, if they kept it, it was to put haircloth under it, or to take on them a rule of life, while to the world they looked as before. . . . And who was he, I say, all the while, but an humble priest, a stranger in Rome, with no distinction of family or letters, no claim of station or of office, great simply in the attraction with which a Divine Power had gifted him? and yet thus humble, thus unennobled, thus empty-handed, he has achieved the glorious title of Apostle of Rome." No apology is necessary for dwelling so long on the character of St. Philip Neri, because it is only by understanding something of that character that Dr. Newman himself can be fully understood.

The first home of the Oratory, in 1848, was in Alcester Street, Birmingham, and amongst its earliest inmates

F

were Ambrose St. John, Gordon, and Henry Austin Mills. "Their long black cloaks," says a local chronicler, referring to the priests of the Oratory generally, "and the peculiar habit of the Order, were conspicuous objects in the streets until the fulmination of an edict against them by the Government, in 1852, incidental to the agitation on the Papal Aggression movement." According to Dr. Ullathorne, the original plan of the Oratory did not contemplate any parochial work, but the Fathers could not see "so many souls in want of pastors" without straining all their efforts in coming to their help. "The Mission in Alcester Street," he says in a letter of approbation to Dr. Newman, "its church and schools, were the first work of the Birmingham Oratory. After several years of close and hard work, and a considerable call upon the private resources of the Fathers who had established this congregation, it was delivered over to other hands, and the Fathers removed to the district of Edgbaston, where, up to that time, nothing Catholic had appeared."

"Father" Newman, as he had now come to be commonly called, by the general public as well as by his own people, had entered upon his new life with a humility which probably astonished some of those who knew him only as a warlike champion of whatever cause he espoused. He toiled at the mission-work as the humblest Friar would have toiled. Into the dens and stews of the great town of Birmingham he and his co-workers plunged with fearless courage and unquenchable zeal. In 1849, when the cholera was raging at Bilston, the local Catholic priest was prostated by his incessant labours, day and night, and it became necessary to find a temporary substitute. Dr. Ullathorne, the Bishop of the diocese, had no other priest to send to take his place in the perilous and urgent work of attending the sick. On hearing of this state of things, Dr. Newman himself, with Father Ambrose and another of the priests of the Oratory, volunteered to take the place of danger, and left the duties of his comparatively quiet home in the Alcester Street Mission house, in order to submit to the discomforts of a hastily improvised accommodation at the priest's house at Bilston. All the rest of the time during which the pestilence was raging, these devoted men were to be seen in the filthiest hovels, amidst the most sordid and sickening surroundings, exposed to the poisonous breath of infection, nobly carrying the message of mercy to the victims of the dread epidemic. Nor were they by any means singular examples of self-devotion. Wherever the cholera broke out, there the Catholic priests were at work, doing their duty fearlessly and in accordance with the sacrificing spirit of their religion. One may dissent altogether from the principles of their faith,—one may even hold that faith to be a superstition and an error,—but one cannot refuse a warm tribute of admiration to the sublime heroism of these pious men. It is a noteworthy episode in the life of Dr. Newman, that, when there was danger to be faced, instead of deputing it to another, he bravely undertook the perilous duty himself. There

are many incidents in his long life which challenge
applause, but none which command it more fully than
this. It was a splendid illustration of the doctrine of
works,—a noble example of that spirit of self-regard-
lessness which is one of the characteristics of the
Roman Catholic clergy all the world over.

Dr. Newman in 1850 founded the Brompton Oratory,
but though it owed to him its "characteristic excel-
lences," his direct connection with it was of the briefest
kind. Its headship and government passed into other
hands, and work of a larger scope and more important
character awaited its founder. The Oratorians, in 1852,
erected a large and commodious building in Hagley
Road, Edgbaston, to which is attached a Church
dedicated to "Our Blessed Lady of the Immaculate
Conception." The building itself is not pretentious,
or even prepossessing, in its architectural features.
It has been described by a graphic writer as "an ugly
red-brick building, shaped in the most modern
of modern styles, in a suburb full of other ugly red-
brick buildings, with a narrow strip of ground before it
planted with dingy shrubs, standing back a little
from the street as if overshadowed by the grandeur
of the neighbouring inn." Here Dr. Newman has
spent, with the exception of a few years in Dublin, the
last thirty years of his life. Here he formed around
him that faithful and affectionate circle of priests many
of whose names are held in high esteem by their
co-religionists—Edward Caswall, the graceful poet,
Ambrose St. John, Henry Bittleston, William P. Neville,

and Henry Ignatius Dudley Ryder. With some of these
—notably with Ambrose St. John—his intimacy was of
the closest kind. These two were for many years
as inseparable as the friends of classic fable, and
when the long and affectionate companionship was
severed by the hand of death, the grief felt by Dr.
Newman was of no common kind. At the funeral of
Father Ambrose, at Rednal—the burial-place of the
Oratorians—his surviving friend was deeply moved.

At the Edgbaston Oratory, somewhat later, Dr. Newman established a school for the education of the sons of
the Catholic gentry. The present Duke of Norfolk, the
head of the Catholic laity in England, was one of his
later pupils, and other scions of noble houses owe their
careful scholarship and admirable moral discipline to
his erudition and conscientious superintendence. In
addition to the Convent and the school, a numerous congregation gathered and grew in the Oratory, and schools
for the poor and other pious institutions have sprung up
in connection with it. Very soon after the establish-
ment of the Edgbaston Oratory, high authority assigned
to Dr. Newman the important work of founding an
Irish Catholic University in Dublin. For a period of
seven years he held the office of Rector in this new
scheme, and guided its steps and watched over its
movements with parental solicitude. The magnitude
and importance of the work are well set forth by the
Bishop of Birmingham: "After the Universities had
been lost to the Catholics of these kingdoms for three
centuries, everything had to be begun from the begin-

ning : the idea of such an institution to be inculcated, the plan to be formed that would work, the resources to be gathered, and the staff of superiors and professors to be brought together. Your name," he says to Dr. Newman, " was then the chief point of attraction which brought these elements together. You alone know what difficulties you had to conciliate, and what to surmount, before the work reached that state of consistency and promise which enabled you to return to those responsibilities in England which you had never laid aside or suspended." Dr. Newman has frequently alluded, in later years, to the universal kindness which he met with in the Sister Isle, a kindness which lightened his anxieties, even if it did not lessen the responsibility of his task. The task was, indeed, a great one. Despite the prestige of his name, and the zeal which he threw into the work, the University never achieved a great measure of success. In the opinion of some it was undertaken under impossible conditions In the opinion of others, among whom is Dr. Newman himself, a future is yet in store for it. In reply to a deputation from the University which tendered him a congratulatory address in 1879, referring to his efforts for the advancement of the University education of Irish Catholics, his lectures on the scope and nature of University education, and the great work he had accomplished as Rector in moulding their newly-formed University, he said that he still cherished a hope of the ultimate success of the scheme. His labours were not unfruitful in a literary sense. The addresses just referred to assumed a more permanent as well as a more elaborate shape in the well-known *Lectures on University Subjects.* He wrote, too, a series of papers originally published in the Dublin *Catholic University Gazette,* in 1854. They were afterwards brought together in one volume, under the title of *The Office and Work of Universities;* and in 1872 appeared in his "Historical Sketches," under the more appropriate title of *The Rise and Progress of Universities.* This work is rich in learning, full of illustration, and graphic in its narrative portion. It gives, from the author's point of view, not only a very comprehensive survey of the historical growth of Universities, but a clear and able exposition of what should be their aim, what faults have hindered their work, and what results are within reach of their attainment. The concluding passage is full of sanguine hope for the future of the Irish Catholic University, whose success was, in its Rector's opinion, presaged " by its triumph over the difficulties of its commence-ment."

Dr. Newman returned from Dublin to the Oratory. He was obliged to do so by the necessities of his congre-gation there. " Everybody can understand," he once said, " what a difficulty it is for a body to be with-out its head, and I only engaged for seven years because I could not otherwise fulfil the charge which the Holy Father had put upon me in the Oratory." The Oratory has been his home ever since, and will be for the rest of his life. When, a score of years later,

he received the Cardinalate, the Pope, in consideration of his great age, gave him permission to reside
where he liked, knowing full well it was the old
man's wish to end his days among the confraternity
with whom he had long been in such close
spiritual communion and personal friendship. Some of
his most notable works have been penned in his rooms
at Edgbaston. There he has worked, and studied, and
written, and prayed with unflagging industry, and a
never-wavering devotion.

CHAPTER V.

THE ANTI-POPERY FEELING—FATHER ACHILLI'S LECTURES—NEW-
MAN'S LECTURES ON "THE PRESENT POSITION OF THE CATHOLICS
IN THIS COUNTRY"—HIS ATTACK ON ACHILLI—CRIMINAL PRO-
CEEDINGS FOR LIBEL—THE TRIAL—INTENSITY OF RELIGIOUS
FEELING— EVIDENCE FOR THE DEFENCE—ACHILLI'S APPEAR-
ANCE IN THE WITNESS BOX—VERDICT FOR THE CROWN—A MIS-
CARRIAGE OF JUSTICE—SENTENCE OF THE COURT—COST OF THE
PROCEEDINGS.

IN the year 1850, the *odium theologicum* between the
Evangelical and the Roman schools reached its sharpest
point of friction. The rival theologies arrayed
against each other all the weapons of a bitter controversy and a seemingly irreconcilable hatred.
There prevailed among the Evangelical party a

great dread of the encroachments of the Holy See. These were the days of the so-called Papal Aggression. Lord John Russell wrote his famous Durham Letter, and a little later on brought in and carried that legislative *brutum fulmen*, the Ecclesiastical Titles Act, which became a dead letter almost as soon as it was passed. Every "'vert" was regarded with holy horror and pious dread. The peculiar waistcoat of the High Church clergyman became known, in the *argot* of the tailor's trade, as the M. B. waistcoat, which mysterious letters were intended to signify "the Mark of the Beast." All that savoured of, or tended to Romanism, was the object, not only of reasonable reprobation, but of violent abuse. Rome itself was even more fiercely assailed. Genuine Protestants, alarmed at the insidious growth of Popery, entered upon an active crusade against its doctrine, its methods, and its corruptions. Their enterprise was supplemented by the active assistance of certain "converted" Romanists, whose unsparing denunciations of the "abominations" of the Church from which they had seceded, helped to feed the prejudices, and intensify the bigotry, of the ultra-Protestant party. Among these was a Doctor Giovanni Giacinto Achilli, who was formerly a friar of the Dominican order, but had fallen under the displeasure of the Papal authorities, had been imprisoned in the dungeons of the Inquisition, and on regaining his liberty had made a profession of the Protestant faith. He threw himself into his new vocation with conspicuous zeal. He came to England and speedily

attracted attention.   An eloquent preacher, a fierce
hater, and a relentless enemy of the religion whose
cloth he had once worn, he attracted crowds of people
wherever he went, and fanned the passions of the anti-
Roman feeling to a white heat of indignation, by
describing the wrongs which he said he had suffered,
the despotic acts of the Inquisition, and the iniquities
of the priesthood.   Over the antecedents of this
quondam friar there hung the shadow of grave scandals.
Ugly stories concerning him found their way into
print.   In the *Dublin Review* for June, 1850, there
appeared an article, generally attributed to Cardinal
Wiseman, in which charges of the most shameless
profligacy were made against Achilli, and with a
particularisation of detail which suggested the necessity
of something more than a flat denial.   He did not,
however, do more at that time than give them a flat
denial, attributing the " slanders " to the malice of his
enemies, and asserting that the enormities alleged
against him were the outcome of a diabolical conspiracy
on the part of unscrupulous persecutors.

    There can be little doubt that Achilli was nearly
if not quite as bad as he was painted.   In 1842 he
left his convent at Viterbo and fled with his mistress to
Corfu, where they lived under the protection of
England.   When the ill-fated brothers Bandiera organ-
ised their expedition into the Kingdom of Naples, they
formed their plans in the house of Achilli, consigning
to him all their valuables, whether of clothing or of
jewellery.   He did not await their being shot to lay

hands on their property. Two days after they had set out it was known that he had sold the greater part of it, and he even strutted about the streets dandified with the raiment of the youths who had gone to shed their blood in the cause of redeeming Italy. These things and worse were openly alleged against him, yet people flocked to hear him preach, and attributed the scandals to the malice of his enemies, the Roman priests.

A year after the appearance of the article in the *Dublin Review*, Dr. Newman began, in Birmingham, a course of lectures on "The Present Position of the Catholics in this Country." These lectures attracted, alike through the eminence of their author and the burning interest of the subject he discussed, an unusual degree of attention. Dr. Newman wore on the platform the habit of the Oratorians. A local historian says : "The Corn Exchange was crowded ; and all who heard those extraordinary utterances, however much they might differ from some of the statements made and the conclusions arrived at, will never forget the rich literary treat which they had on the occasion. The bursts of fervid eloquence, the sparkling flashes of wit, the passages of keen irony, the subtle though often deceptive logic, the deep sincerity and the earnest piety of the speaker, all combined to produce an effect upon the mind of the hearer which can never entirely pass away. Those who heard the lectures will recall the pleasure of those evenings as they read them now; but to those who did not hear them, the published volume is no more than the letter of a correspondent whom they have never seen and whose voice they have never heard, as compared with the letter of a departed friend whose very look and accent is in the words which they read." The fifth lecture was devoted to a consideration of " The Logical Inconsistency of the Protestant View." In the course of it, Dr. Newman vindicated the Church of his adoption from the aspersions of Achilli. He attacked this person with unsparing severity. It was as if he used the lightning for a whip, so terrible and scathing was the quality of his scorn. Achilli, he said, was in no sense a real convert, but having been expelled from the Roman Church for his scandalous conduct, had adopted Protestantism from the exigency of the moment. In the course of a denunciation which lost nothing of its effect from being delivered in a silvery sweetness of voice and a subdued manner, Newman used the following language :—

" And in the midst of outrages such as these, wiping its mouth, and clasping its hands, and turning up its eyes, it trudges to the Town Hall to hear Dr. Achilli expose the Inquisition ! Ah ! Dr. Achilli ; I might have spoken of him last week had time admitted of it. The Protestant world flocks to hear him because he has something to tell of the Catholic Church. He has something to tell, it is true ; he *has* a scandal to reveal, he *has* an argument to exhibit. It is a simple one, and a powerful one, as far as it goes —and it is *one.* That one argument is himself ; it is his presence which is the triumph of Protestants ; it is the sight of him which is a Catholic's confusion. It is, indeed, a confusion that our Holy Mother could have had a priest like him. He feels the force of the argument, and he shows himself to the multitude that is gazing upon him. ' Mothers of families,' he seems to say, ' gentle maidens, innocent children, look at me, for I am worth looking at. You do not see such a sight every day. Can any Church live over the imputation of such a production as I am ? I have been a Roman priest and a hypocrite ; I have been a profligate under a cowl. I am that Father Achilli who, as early as 1826, was deprived of my faculty to lecture, for an offence which my superiors did their best to conceal; and who in 1827 had already earned the reputation of a scandalous Friar. I am that Achilli who, in the diocese of Viterbo, in February, 1831, robbed of her honour a young woman of 18; who, in September, 1833, was found guilty of a second such crime, in the case of a person 28; and who perpetrated a third in July, 1834, in the case of another aged 24. I am he who was afterwards found guilty of sins, similar or worse, in other towns of the neighbourhood. I am that son of St. Dominic who is known to have repeated the offence at Capua, in 1834 and 1835, and at Naples again in 1840, in the case of a child of 15. I am he who chose the sacristy of the church for one of these crimes, and Good Friday for another. Look on me, ye mothers of England, a confessor against Popery, for 'Ye ne'er may look upon my like again.' I am that veritable priest who, after all this, began to speak against, not only the Catholic faith, but the moral law, and perverted others by my teaching. I am the Cavaliere Achilli who then went to Corfu, made the wife of a tailor faithless to her husband, and lived publicly and travelled about with the wife of a chorus singer. I am that Professor in the Protestant College at Malta who, with two others, was dismissed from my post for offences which the authorities could not get themselves to describe. And now, attend to me, such as I am, and you shall see what you shall see about the barbarity and profligacy of the inquisitors of Rome.' You speak truly, O Achilli, and we cannot answer you a word. You are a priest; you have been a Friar; you, it is undeniable, are the scandal of Catholicism, and the palmary argument of Protestants, by your extraordinary depravity. You have been, it is true, a profligate, an unbeliever, and a hypocrite. You are reported in an official document of the Neapolitan police to be 'known for habitual incontinency;' your name came before the Civil Tribunal of Corfu for your crime and adultery. You have put the crown on your offences by, as long as you could, denying them all; you have professed to seek after truth, when you were ravening after sin. Yes, you are an incontrovertible proof that priests may fall, and friars break their vows. You are your own witness; but while you *need* not go out of yourself for your argument, neither are you *able.* With you the argument begins; with you, too, it ends: the beginning and the ending you are both."

Dr. Newman concluded his discourse with the statement that Achilli was not mad, but that worse than mad were those who gave ear to him. The lectures, including this tremendous indictment, were subsequently published, and Dr. Achilli found it imperative, in the face of such specific charges, to put his assailant to the proof. Criminal proceedings for libel were taken against the publishers, but, on Dr. Newman's frank and ready admission of the authorship, were at once transferred to him. The trial came on before Lord Campbell on June 21st, 1852, and lasted several days. The Attorney-General was the leading counsel for the prosecution, and Sir Alexander Cockburn for the defence. The defendant pleaded "Not guilty" and justification, and set up twenty-three distinct charges in support of the allegations contained in the libel. Rarely has a case excited profounder interest or aroused stronger prejudices. Every day the Court was crowded to inconvenience. Religious feeling ran high. It was evident from the outset that the majority of those who succeeded in gaining admission were animated by a full share of Protestant zeal. At any more than ordinarily vehement thrust at Rome, the Court rang with applause. Men seemed to forget that they were in a Court of Justice, and hot, if not passionate, antipathies found frequent vent in unseemly manifestations. Popular feeling was entirely with the prosecutor. He was regarded by the majority as the victim of a malicious plot. Rome, it was argued, was annoyed at his disclosures and afraid of his influence, and had resolved upon crushing him, no matter what the means. Dr. Newman seems to have been regarded as a sort of unwitting tool in the matter. No one who knew aught of his high character, and the unsullied purity of his motives, would have suspected him for a moment of complicity in any such base designs. But he was thought to have rashly taken up the weapons artfully put to his hand, and to have lent his high sanction to charges, of the truth or falsehood of which he could have had no personal knowledge. In a measure, no doubt, this was true. His evidence for the crimes of which he accused Dr. Achilli could have been, at the best, only hearsay evidence. The sincerity of his belief in that evidence could not get rid of the fact that he had echoed and repeated charges of the origin of which he could have known nothing save by report.

It would be impossible to reproduce here the evidence given in the course of the hearing. A number of women came forward and solemnly swore to acts of the grossest immorality on the part of the prosecutor. Peasants from Italy and domestic servants in London asseverated that they had been the victims of his unbridled lust. If a tithe of what they said was true, this Achilli must have been one of the vilest men who ever proved that *cucullus non facit monachum*. Most of the witnesses were now married, and it was argued by the counsel for the defence that they were not likely to have come forward with these stories concerning their own shame unless they had been true. Evidence was also given of the judgment of the Inquisition, whereby, on the ground of such charges, the prosecutor was deprived of all ecclesiastical functions for ever, and sent to a con-

vent for three years. But when the prosecutor was put
into the box he gave every statement made by the
women a point-blank denial. His evidence comprised
an account of his life from the age of sixteen, when he
entered the Dominican order, to his marriage at Rome in
1849, when he had ceased to be a priest of the Church
of Rome. He not only denied the acts of immorality
with which he was charged, but stated that it was
entirely on questions of doctrine that he had been
cited before the Inquisition. His appearance at the
trial is thus described by a contemporary chronicler:—
"He is a plain-featured, middle-sized man, about 50
years of age, and his face is strongly Italian. His forehead is low and receding, his nose prominent, the mouth
and the muscles around it full of resolution and courage.
He wears a black wig, the hair of which is perfectly
straight, and, being close shaved, this wig gives to his
appearance a certain air of the conventicle. Yet he
retains many traces of the Roman Catholic priest,
especially in his bearing, enunciation, and gestures,
which have a sort of stealthy grace about them. His
eyes are deep-set and lustrous, and with his black hair,
dark complexion, and sombre, demure aspect, leave an
impression upon the mind of the observer by no means
agreeable, and not readily to be forgotten. The questions put to him by his own counsel he answered with
great clearness, and in a calm, unwavering, quiet
manner, without any trace of strong excitement, or
feelings deeply roused. Sometimes a slight, con-
temptuous smile accompanied his denials of opposing

evidence, and once or twice he even seemed to treat points merrily. Yet at certain portions of his examination, without losing his self-possession, he became more animated. His dark, sunken eyes flashed fire as he listened and replied to the questions put. This was particularly the case when he was cross-examined by Sir Alexander Cockburn on the more material points of the libel, and especially when he was confronted by the Italian women who had sworn that he debauched them. The effect produced by these meetings was quite dramatic, the poor women eyeing their alleged seducer with half-timid, yet steady glances, while he, his face overcome for the moment with a slight pallor, turned upon them looks that seemed to pierce through them."

The emphatic denials of Dr. Achilli brought the issue, as Dr. Newman's counsel pointed out, to one of deliberate perjury on one side or the other. No man could have acted as he was alleged to have acted, and have forgotten all about it. No woman could have been under a delusion with regard to what the witnesses advanced. Either he was a consummate liar, or they were consummate liars. It was for the jury to decide which was entitled to credence. Sir A. Cockburn's speech for the defence was a masterly and brilliant effort of forensic oratory. He besought the jury to dismiss from their minds everything in the shape of theological bias, and to deal with the case on its merits, and on its natural and unstrained probabilities. The jury, however, were seemingly too much carried

G

away by their religious prepossessions to believe the irresistible evidence advanced in support of the plea of justification. Of the twenty-three justificatory charges, they only found for the defendant on one, namely, that Dr. Archilli had been deprived of his professorship and prohibited from preaching. The others, they said, were not proved to their satisfaction. This was equivalent, of course, to a verdict for the Crown. They expressly stated that they had come to their decision apart from any reference to the question of Protestantism or Catholicism. However that may have been, the atmosphere of the whole proceedings was clouded with theological prejudice. The judge himself "thanked God" that there was no Inquisition in England, or ever likely to be one; and the applause evoked by this extra-judicial utterance passed without any rebuke.

Impartial men, accustomed to weigh evidence, felt satisfied that the verdict involved a grave miscarriage of justice. Even the *Times*, notwithstanding its Protestant leanings, spoke out strongly, and declared that the result of the trial would deal a terrible blow to the administration of justice in England, and that Roman Catholics would have good cause for the future to assert that here there is no justice for them, whenever litigation turns on a cause which arouses the Protestant passions of judges and juries.

Later on in the year the Court of Queen's Bench granted a rule for a new trial on the ground that the verdict was against evidence, but no further action was taken, and on January 29th, 1853, Dr. Newman came up for judgment. Mr. Justice Coleridge, in giving utterance to the finding of the Court, expressed its conviction that Dr. Newman honestly believed the truth of the allegations he made against Dr. Achilli, and that he did not compose and publish the libel from personal malice, but because Dr. Achilli had assailed a religion he held dear, and had done so in Birmingham, where it was extremely important his authority should not be lessened.   Still, it was not to be denied that he had repeated the offensive expressions as if they were matter for exultation and merriment, and, as it would appear, with utter recklessness of their great importance and serious nature.   "Firmly attached as I am, and I believe ever shall be, to the Church of England, in which I have lived, and in which I hope to die, yet there is nothing on my mind, on seeing you before me, but the deepest regret.   I can hardly expect that you will take in good part many of the observations I have felt it my duty to make.   Suffer me, however, to say one or two words more.   The great controversy between the Churches will go on, we know not, through God's pleasure, how long.   Whether, henceforward you will take any part in it or not, it will be for you to determine; but I think the pages before me should give you this warning, upon calm consideration, that if you engage in this controversy, you should engage in it neither personally nor bitterly.   The best road to unity is by increase of holiness of life.   If you for the future sustain, as you may think you are bound to do, by your publications, the cause of the Church of Rome, I entreat you to do it in a spirit of charity, in a spirit of humility, in a spirit worthy of your great abilities, of your ardent piety, of your holy life, and of our common Christianity. The sentence of the Court is that you pay to her Majesty a fine of £100, and that you be imprisoned in the first class of misdemeanants in the Queen's Prison until the fine be paid." The fine was instantly paid, and Dr. Newman left the Court. The expenses of the trial had been enormous, the defendant's bill of costs amounting to £12,000. He was not however, called upon to pay this ruinous sum himself. Catholics in all parts of the world contributed to his defence, and showed by their material aid their profound belief in the substantial accuracy of his charges against Achilli.

CHAPTER VI.

An Important Epoch—Canon Kingsley's Accusation—Newman's Correspondence with Messrs. Macmillan and Mr. Kingsley—"The Word of a Professor of Lying that he does not Lie"—"What, then, does Dr. Newman mean?"—Kingsley's View of the Controversy—The "Apologia pro Vita sua"—Sensation caused by it—Change in the Attitude of the Protestant Public—Congratulations of the Catholic Priesthood—Newman as a Poet—"The Dream of Gerontius"—Rumours and Contradiction—Ungrateful Criticisms—Address of Sympathy at Stafford—Newman's References to Misrepresentation.

WE now come to a most important epoch in Dr. Newman's life. Up to this time he had never been quite rightly understood by his Protestant fellow countrymen. They had an undefined suspicion that he had somehow played them false. It remained for Canon Kingsley to give him the opportunity of putting on record such a defence of his conversion as satisfied his most bitter opponents of the thorough sincerity of every step he had taken. It came about in this wise. Mr. Kingsley, although a very honest and honourable clergyman, was not remarkable for controversial prudence, and now and then allowed his polemical zeal to betray him into exaggerated or incorrect statements. In a review of J. A. Froude's "History of England," in

Macmillan's Magazine for January, 1864, speaking of the Roman Catholics and the virtue of truth, he said, in his impetuous way, "Truth, for its own sake, had never been a virtue with the Roman clergy. Father Newman informs us that it need not, and on the whole ought not to be; that cunning is the weapon which Heaven has given to the saints wherewith to withstand the brute male force of the wicked world which marries and is given in marriage. Whether his notion be doctrinally correct or not, it is at least historically so." There was no justification for this amazing attack. As Mr. J. A. Froude says:—" Kingsley, in truth, entirely misunderstood Newman's character. Newman's whole life had been a struggle for truth. He had neglected his own interests; he had never thought of them at all. He had brought to bear a most powerful and subtle intellect to support the convictions of a conscience which was superstitiously sensitive. His single object had been to discover what were the real relations between man and his Maker, and to shape his own conduct by the conclusions at which he arrived. To represent such a person as careless of truth was neither generous nor even reasonable." Perhaps, too, it may be said with equal truth that Newman misunderstood Kingsley. The latter had read Dr. Newman's views about miracles and had come to the conclusion that " the methods of his reasoning confounded his perceptions of truth." But the accusation was so nakedly and inconsiderately worded that one cannot wonder at Father Newman feeling himself wounded by it. He at

once wrote to the publishers, pointing out that there
was no reference at the foot of the page to any words of
his, much less any quotation from his writings, in
support of it. He did not write to expostulate or to
seek reparation. He did but wish to draw the attention
of Messrs. Macmillan, as gentlemen, to a grave and
gratuitous slander, with which he "felt confident they
would be sorry to find their name associated." The
letter was shown to Mr. Kingsley who wrote Dr.
Newman to the following effect:—"That my words were
just, I believed from many passages of your writings;
but the document to which I expressly referred was
one of your Sermons on 'Subjects of the Day,' No.
XX., in the volume published in 1844, and entitled
'Wisdom and Innocence.' I am most happy to hear
from you that I mistook (as I understand from your
letter) your meaning; and I shall be most happy, on
your showing me that I have wronged you, to retract
my accusation as publicly as I have made it."
Dr. Newman acknowledged the receipt of this, and
said "when I received your letter, taking upon yourself
the authorship [of the obnoxious review] I was
amazed." That he felt most deeply the reflection cast
upon his regard for veracity is shown by a letter to a
mutual friend, who had interposed with the laudable
object of bringing about an amicable understanding.
He demanded an explanation, and an admission that the
accusation in the review was without justification.
Canon Kingsley submitted the draft of a paragraph
which he proposed to insert in the next number of the

Magazine. "Dr. Newman," it ran, "has, by letter, expressed in the strongest terms, his denial of the meaning which I had put upon his words. No man knows the use of words better than Dr. Newman; no man, therefore, has a better right to define what he does, or does not, mean by them. It only remains, therefore, for me to express my hearty regret at having so seriously mistaken him; and my hearty pleasure at finding him on the side of Truth, in this, or any other matter." The impartial reader must admit that these admissions were so worded as to induce an interpretation, in the popular mind, not altogether favourable to Dr. Newman. This he clearly saw, and withheld from the explanation the approbation he would fain have bestowed. Mr. Kingsley then offered to omit the expressions "No man knows the use of words better than Dr. Newman," and, "my hearty pleasure at finding him on the side of Truth, in this, or any other, matter." He considered that having done this he had "done as much as one English gentleman could expect from another." It was not, however, sufficient for Dr. Newman, who contended that what was left "would be understood by the general reader as implying that he had been confronted with definite extracts from his works," and had laid before the publishers his own interpretation of them. Such a proceeding he had, he said, challenged, but had not been so fortunate as to bring about. Mr. Kingsley's proposed reparation was "decidedly not" sufficient. It was, however, inserted in the Magazine without any farther material alteration, and elicited from Dr. Newman a crushing and ironical rejoinder. It is such a splendid specimen of his pitiless controversial skill and brilliancy of expression that no apology is needed for giving a lengthy extract from it:—

"Mr. Kingsley begins then by exclaiming,—'O the chicanery, the wholesale fraud, the vile hypocrisy, the conscience-killing tyranny of Rome! We have not far to seek for an evidence of it. There's Father Newman to wit: one living specimen is worth a hundred dead ones. He, a Priest writing of Priests, tells us that lying is never any harm.'

I interpose : 'You are taking a most extraordinary liberty with my name. If I have said this, tell me when and where.'

Mr. Kingsley replies: 'You said it, Reverend Sir, in a Sermon which you preached when a Protestant, as Vicar of St. Mary's, and published in 1844; and I could read you a very salutary lecture on the effects which that Sermon had at the time on my own opinion of you.'

I make answer : 'Oh . . . *Not*, it seems, as a Priest speaking of Priests ; but let us have the passage.'

Mr. Kingsley relaxes : 'Do you know, I like your *tone*. From your *tone* I rejoice, greatly rejoice, to be able to believe that you did not mean what you said.'

I rejoin : ' *Mean* it! I maintain I never *said* it, whether as a Protestant or as a Catholic.'

Mr. Kingsley replies : 'I waive that point.'

I object : 'Is it possible ! What ? Waive the main question ! I either said it or I didn't. You have made a monstrous charge against me ; direct, distinct, public. You are bound to prove it as directly, as distinctly, as publicly ; or to own you can't.'

'Well,' says Mr. Kingsley, 'if you are quite sure you did not say it, I'll take your word for it ; I really will.'

My *word* ! I am dumb. Somehow I thought that it was my *word* that happened to be on trial. The *word* of a Professor of lying, that he does not *lie* !

But Mr. Kingsley reassures me : 'We are both gentlemen,' he says, 'I have done as much as one English gentleman can expect from another.'

I begin to see : he thought me a gentleman at the very time that he said I taught lying on system. After all, it is not I, but it is Mr.

Kingsley who did not mean what he said. 'Habemus confitentem reum.'

So we have confessedly come round to this, preaching without practising; the common theme of satirists from Juvenal to Walter Scott! "I left Baby Charles and Steenie laying his duty before him,' says King James of the reprobate Dalgarno: 'O Geordie, jingling Geordie, it was grand to hear Baby Charles laying down the guilt of dissimulation, and Steenie lecturing on the turpitude of incontinence.'"

Canon Kingsley was completely worsted; the weak spots in his armour had been found out, he was pierced through and through. He might have exclaimed, in the words, if not in the spirit, of Sir Andrew Aguecheek, that had he known his adversary to be so "cunning of fence" he would never have challenged him. Newman's pitiless logic left him in a sorry plight. Yet he returned, like the doughty knight that he was, to the combat. He discussed the question in a pamphlet, *What, then, does Dr. Newman mean?*— a pamphlet not to be commended for its temper, or for its taste. There was plenty of hard hitting in it, but the hitting, to use a sporting term, was somewhat wild; there were plenty of strong epithets and condemnatory terms, and insinuations of dishonesty; and the whole of Dr. Newman's career seemed to be distinctly challenged, and his sincerity impugned. It would be profitless now to go over the arguments in detail, or to examine the caustic and effective passages of Dr. Newman's reply. That reply was one of the most memorable episodes in literature,—the *Apologia pro Vitâ suâ.* In it he laid bare his soul to the whole world, and in spite of a natural sensitiveness which must have made him shrink from the task, gave a full and complete history of his religious opinions from childhood to the period of his entry into the Roman Communion.

Before dismissing Kingsley's part in this new chapter of the " Quarrels of Authors," it is but fair to add that he was to the last, of opinion that, as regards the policy of Rome, he was in the right after all. On this point, an extract from the valuable Memoirs edited by his widow cannot fail to be of interest:— " This fact may be mentioned, that information conveyed to Mr. Kingsley that Dr. Newman was in bad health, depressed, and averse from polemical discussion, coupled with Dr. Newman's own words in the early part of the correspondence, in which he seemed to deprecate controversy, appealed irresistibly to Mr. Kingsley's consideration, and put him to a great disadvantage in the issue. Still throughout there were many who held with him—among them some personal friends in the Roman Catholic Church. Many private letters, too, of generous sympathy from strangers came to cheer him on—some from laymen—some from clergymen—some even from working men, who having come in contact with the teaching of Roman Catholic priests, knew the truth of Mr. Kingsley's statements. Last but not least, a pamphlet was published by the Rev. Frederick Meyrick, entitled, *But is not Kingsley right after all?* This pamphlet was never answered. For the right understanding of this controversy, it cannot be too strongly insisted upon, that it was for truth and truth only that Mr. Kingsley craved and had fought. The main point at issue was not the personal integrity of Dr. Newman, but the question whether the Roman Catholic priesthood are encouraged or discouraged to pursue 'Truth for its own sake.' While no one more fully acknowledged the genius and power of his opponent than Mr. Kingsley himself, or was more ready to confess that he had 'crossed swords with one who was too strong for him,' yet he always felt that the general position which he had taken up against the policy of the Roman Catholic Church remained unshaken. 'It was his righteous indignation,' says Dean Stanley, 'against what seemed to him the glorification of a tortuous and ambiguous policy, which betrayed him into the only personal controversy in which he was ever entangled, and in which, matched in unequal conflict with the most subtle and dexterous controversialist of modern times, it is not surprising that for the moment he was apparently worsted, whatever we may think of the ultimate issues that were raised in the struggle, and whatever may be the total results of our experiences, before and after, on the main question over which the combat was fought—on the relation of the human conscience to truth or to authority.'"

It would be impossible to exaggerate the effect of the *Apologia* upon the public mind. It came out in parts, and each new part was looked forward to with eager interest. With the third part the work became purely autobiographical. The writer unveiled his life, his opinions, the influences which had operated upon him, the changes he had undergone, with a candour that carried conviction in every quarter. He traced his childish prejudices, his Oxford beliefs, and the progress of his conversion, with minute and unreserved freedom. He threw, as it were, the lime-light upon his intellectual nature, analysed his own motives, explained his own beliefs and his reasons for holding them. As a psychological study,—as a remarkable example of searching and faithful introspection, the *Apologia* will take its place among the English classics. No more acute self-analysis had ever been unreservedly communicated to the world. A thoughtful critic says of it, " as an autobiography, in the highest sense of that word, as the portraiture that is, and record of what the man was, irrespective of those common accidents of humanity which too often load the biographer's pages, it is eminently dramatic. Hardly do the *Confessions of St. Augustine* more vividly reproduce the old African Bishop before successive generations in all the greatness and struggles of his life than do these pages the very inner being of this remarkable man—' the living intelligence ' as he describes it, ' by which I write, and argue, and act.' There is in these pages an absolute revealing of the hidden life in its acting, and its processes, which at times is almost startling, which is everywhere of the deepest interest." In some respects it would not be difficult to draw a parallel between Newman and Dante. The pages of both are imbued with scholastic theology. It has been acutely pointed out that there

is in the *Apologia* something analagous (in all but the
entire absence of a Beatrice) to the *Vita Nuova* and
the *De Monarchia*. " There is the same unveiling of
the secrets of the heart, the same pursuit of an ideal
Church and an ideal State.   Apart from the introspec-
tive searchingness of the *Apologia*, it was written in
such a charming style, in such melodious and perfect
English, that people unused to doctrinal arguments,
and, like Gallio, caring for none of these things,
found themselves awaiting with eager interest the
issue of each successive number.   The keynote of
the work was a determination to be the victim
of Protestant misrepresentation no longer.   " I
must," said Dr. Newman, " give the true key to
my whole life ; I must show what I am that it
may be seen what I am not, and that the phantom
may be extinguished which gibbers instead of me.
I wish to be known as a living man, and not as a
scarecrow which is dressed up in my clothes.   False
ideas may be refuted indeed by argument, but by true
ideas alone are they expelled.   .   .   .   I will draw
out, as far as may be, the history of my mind ; I will
state the point at which I began, in what external sug-
gestion or accident each opinion had its rise, how far
and how they were developed from within, how they
grew, were modified, were combined, were in collision
with each other, and were changed ; again, how I conducted myself towards them, and how, and how far, and
for how long a time, I thought I could hold them consistently with ecclesiastical engagements which I had

made, and with the position which I filled." All this
was truly set forth. It is not too much to say that
the effect of the volume, when it was finished, was
to completely change the attitude of the public towards
him. Their suspicion melted away into the thinnest
of thin air. His opponents were forced to the conclusion that they had hitherto misjudged him. The striking
candour of his avowals had all the significance of irre-
fragable proof. People forgot all about the quarrel
with Kingsley in the presence of a larger interest.
Newman himself felt the same thing. "And now," he
says at the end of the first part, "I am in a train of
thought higher and more serene than any which
slanders can disturb. Away with you, Mr. Kingsley,
and fly into space."

The effect of the publication upon members of his
own community may be judged from the fact
that at a Diocesan Synod of Roman Catholic clergy,
held at St. Chad's, Birmingham, in June 1864, an
address was presented to him conveying the hearty
thanks of the Synod for his vindication of the honour
of the Catholic priesthood, and for "the ingenuous
fulness" of his answer to "a false and unprovoked
accusation." In replying to this address, Dr. Newman
said, referring to the incident which had called it forth,
that he had to perform a duty which had been thrust
upon him by circumstances over which he had
no control. If, however, in the vindication of his
character, he had indirectly done good by lessening
prejudice against the Catholic clergy or the faith which

was so dear to them all, he was, of course, deeply grateful for the result. And, in allusion to a hope which had been expressed that he would continue to use his pen in combating errors which assailed the Church, he remarked with a humorous pathos that old age was more for suffering than for action; it was a kind of purgatory in which old men were providentially placed in order that they might learn that it was better to suffer than to do; and his principal business now was to suffer, and to ask their charity for himself in this purgatory. It will be seen, though, as the narrative proceeds that Dr. Newman, though then threescore and three years of age, was neither past the capability nor the will for action; and that if it was part of his lot to suffer, it was no less a part of his duty to do.

The year following the publication of the *Apologia* was rendered interesting by the composition of a work of a totally different kind,—the well-known poem entitled *The Dream of Gerontius.* And here it may not be altogether out of place to introduce one or two general remarks. Dr. Newman's place in literature is to some extent independent of his place as a theologian, notwithstanding that nearly everything he wrote was the outcome of theological studies. As poet, as critic, as historian, as controversialist, all his work was dominated by the religious instinct, and coloured to some extent by his religious prepossessions. Allusions have been made so frequently in these pages to the chief productions of his pen that it is unnecessary here to bring them into court as proofs of this proposition. Theology, in some shape or other, was the basis upon which he constructed his literary work. It was the mainspring of his appearance in the field of literature. Yet it is quite possible to judge of his quality without scrutinising very narrowly the motives which guided him. A work like the *Apologia* can be estimated and valued without our being deeply interested in the eternal rivalries of the Christian churches, possibly even without our having much sympathy with the polemics of either of them. The *Parochial Sermons* do not demand of the reader an acceptance of the Anglican theory before he is able to appreciate the lucidity, the force, the pure English, and the skilful argumentation of those pulpit classics. The *History of the Arians* does not tax the patience of the secular student because it happens to describe the dissensions of the Early Church. So, too, with Dr. Newman's poetry. The sweet fragrance of its devotional spirit and the deep piety of its themes are no hindrances to its enjoyment simply as a literary feast. And here one is struck by the rarity of the combination which is a phenomenal characteristic of Dr. Newman's intellectual gifts. He possesses not only the logical faculty, but the imaginative as well; he is not only a subtle dialectician, but a fascinating singer. The same pen which demolished Canon Kingsley, and which gave Mr. Gladstone something to think over, wrote *The Dream of Gerontius*. This combination of the poetical with the argumentative is the keynote to much of his fascination as a writer. The dry bones of disquisition are habited

H

in comeliness and beauty, and enlivened by the play of a delicate fancy and the graces of a supersubtle wit. The flights of his Muse, on the other hand, are kept in decorous restraint by the modifying influence of the logical mind. In no case does the rhetorical imagination run away with the reins of common-sense, or the "fine frenzy" of the poet lead him into obscurities of expression, or even into momentary forgetfulness of the purity of his English. Dr. Newman's verses possess in a large sense that delightful self-emitting light of intelligibility which characterises his prose writings. Not all of them, perhaps, rise to the height demanded by the standards of true poetry. Here and there one meets with a piece, in the collected edition, which, though faultless in expression and suggestive in scholarship, does not fall upon the ear as if it came hot and hissing from the furnace of the poet's brain. Nor are his verses, as a rule, strikingly harmonious; the metre sometimes halts. None the less, however, is Newman a genuine poet. His hymns are marked by a beautiful subjective feeling, and occasionally by the pathos which is uttered only by those whose hearts have been wrung. They often succeed in burning themselves into the mind of the reader. There are few tenderer, more trustful, or more devotional verses than those of "Lead, kindly Light," which has been fitly characterised by a competent critic as the most popular hymn in the language. Many of the earlier poems are expressions of the moods or thoughts then paramount. Hence we have the frequent doubts, and lamentations, and apprehensions of an on-coming evil, which were the children of his views regarding religious liberalism. Nor is the tone of these rebukeful verses at all times lacking in a combative spirit. The pen seems now and then almost to grow into a sword. The poet not only bewails the offences of the unfaithful, but he smites them hip and thigh when the mood is on him. Writing of England, in 1832, he says:—

> " He who scann'd Sodom for His righteous men
> Still spares thee for thy ten ;
> But, should vain tongues the Bride of Heaven defy,
> He will not pass thee by ;
> For, as earth's kings welcome their spotless guest,
> So gives he them by turn, to suffer or be blest."

It is not, however, with the sentiments of the author so much as with his style that we have to do. It is, perhaps, needless to remark that many of his poems are in the nature of self-communings, and contain passages of prayerful entreaty for larger faith, a fuller measure of righteousness, and a saintlier life. In all, the language is fitly, sometimes exquisitely, chosen. Every line, in fact, is pervaded by a scholarly finish. Some of the matins, lauds, and vespers written by Dr. Newman after he entered the Church of Rome, are perfect examples of a refined hymnody. Take these verses from a *Song for Candlemas* :—

> " We wait along the penance-tide
> Of solemn fast and prayer ;
> While song is hush'd, and lights grow dim
> In the sin-laden air.

> And while the sword in Mary's soul
>   Is driven home, we hide
> In our own hearts, and count the wounds
>   Of passion and of pride."

And for perfect beauty of expression, take these lines on *Heathen Greece*, written in 1856 :—

> " Where are the Islands of the Blest ?
>   They stud the Ægean Sea ;
> And where the deep Elysian rest ?
>   It haunts the vale where Peneus strong
> Pours his incessant stream along,
> While craggy ridge and mountain bare
> Cut keenly through the liquid air,
> And, in their own pure tints array'd,
> Scorn earth's green robes which change and fade,
>   And stand in beauty undecay'd,
>   Guards of the bold and free.
>
> For what is Afric, but the home
>   Of burning Phlegethon ?
> What the low beach and silent gloom,
> And chilling mists of that dull river,
> Along whose bank the thin ghosts shiver,—
> The thin wan ghosts that once were men,—
> But Tauris, isle of moor and fen,
>   Or, dimly traced by seamen's ken,
>   The pale-cliff'd Albion."

The most imaginative of all Dr. Newman's writings is unquestionably *The Dream of Gerontius.* It has been not inaptly described as "the most vivid sketch of things beyond the veil that has been given to the world since Dante." It has, indeed, been remarked by a penetrating critic that Newman, both in this remarkable poem and in some of his contributions to the *Lyra Apostolica*, has thrown in, here and there, some perfectly Dantesque touches. "Tender affection and prophetic sternness, subtle thought and vivid speech, the mingling of beauty, horror, grotesqueness in his vision of the unseen world—these all remind us of the great poem in which the Florentine poet portrayed what lies 'beyond the veil.'"

The death-bed of a dear friend was the inspiring cause which occasioned *The Dream of Gerontius* to be written. Gerontius, while he lies a-dying, dreams of his soul's transportation to the unseen world, and its reception by the ministering agents of the Almighty's will. In a sublime strain of poetic power the mysteries are pictured that lie hidden across the portals of the tomb. The straining eye of a hungering fancy discloses its idea of the " May be " of the soul's future. Meaner imaginations are almost appalled at the boldness of the attempt. An awful realism seems to pervade the picture. The angel and the soul hold dialogues of solemn significance ; demons howl their unholy dissonance ; heavenly choirs hymn their votive praises to the Highest; the souls in purgatory welcome the new comer with a psalm. The language rises to the level of this majestic theme ; the rhythm harmonises with its grandeur. Though they are human words which the angel uses, and human ideas which he expresses with them, it is scarcely hyperbolical to say that the plane of the supernatural seems to have been reached, and an awesomeness given to the utterances in keeping with their character. Note the majestic calm of the explanation in the following extract. The Soul remarks on the powerlessness of the scoffing demons—

> " How impotent they are ! and yet on earth
>   They have repute for wondrous power and skill,
>   And books describe, how that the very face
>   Of the Evil One, if seen, would have a force
>   Even to freeze the blood, and choke the life
>   Of him who saw it."

To which the Angel replies,—

>   " In thy trial-state
>   Thou hadst a traitor nestling close at home,
>   Connatural, who with the powers of hell
>   Was leagued, and of thy senses kept the keys,
>   And to that deadliest foe unlock'd thy heart.
>   And therefore is it, in respect of man,
>   Those fallen ones show so majestical.
>   But, when some child of grace, Angel or Saint,
>   Pure and upright in his integrity
>   Of nature, meets the demons on their raid,
>   They scud away as cowards from the fight.
>   Nay, oft hath holy hermit in his cell,
>   Not yet disburdened of mortality,
>   Mock'd at their threats and warlike overtures ;
>   Or, dying, when they swarmed, like flies, around,
>   Defied them, and departed to his Judge."

Passages even more characteristic of the thrilling
grandeur of a supra-mundane situation follow when the
Soul " with intemperate energy of love, flies to the dear
feet of Emmanuel." With exquisite love and tenderness
the Angel consigns its charge to the penal waters of the
purgatorial state. Whether there be a purgatorial state
or not,—whether prayers for the dead can be of any
avail or not,—are questions which need not interfere
with our appreciation of such beautiful lines as these:—

> " Angels, to whom the willing task is given,
>   Shall tend, and nurse, and lull thee, as thou liest ;
>   And Masses on the earth, and prayers in heaven,
>   Shall aid thee at the throne of the Most Highest.

Farewell, but not for ever! brother dear,
  Be brave and patient on thy bed of sorrow ;
Swiftly shall pass thy night of trial here,
  And I will come and wake thee on the morrow."

The story runs that this sublime composition was so lightly valued by Dr. Newman that he had consigned, or was about to consign, it to the waste-paper basket, when a lucky accident led to its rescue, the quick appreciation of some discriminating critic, and its subsequent publication.

About the year 1862 there were many rumours afloat to the effect that Dr. Newman was unsettled in his views, and that he was not happy in the Church of Rome. These he thought fit to answer by declaring that he had never had one moment of wavering of trust in that Church ever since he had been received into her fold. "Protestants," he added, in a vein of humorous sarcasm, "are always on the look out for some loophole or evasion in a Catholic's statement of fact; therefore, in order to give them full satisfaction if I can, I do hereby profess *ex animo*, with an absolute internal assent and consent, that Protestantism is the dreariest of possible religions; that the thought of the Anglican service makes me shiver, and the thought of the Thirty-nine Articles makes me shudder. Return to the Church of England! No, the net is broken, and we are delivered. I should be a consummate fool (to use a mild term) if in my old age I left the land flowing with milk and honey for the city of confusion and the house of bondage."

His abilities as a controversialist were not long

suffered to rust in idleness. Early in 1866 he answered Dr. Pusey's *Eirenicon*, a proposal for the re-union of Christendom, which he argued to be impossible. About this time Dr. Newman was subjected to a series of ungenerous attacks at the hands of some of his co-religionists. No man had ever done more for his adopted faith than he had, yet there was dissatisfaction rather than gratitude in certain quarters. The excuse for all this was that he was not altogether "sound,"— that he entertained on some points views which were not quite in accord with those of the Ultramontane school. A project which he had in contemplation to found a branch of the Oratory at Oxford fell through, according to the *Guardian*, on account of the opposition of the English Roman Catholic bishops. The opposition may have proceeded from a *bonâ fide* doubt as to the practicability or wisdom of the scheme. At all events, the mooting of the idea led to some acrimonious criticisms in the *Weekly Register*, to the effect that Dr. Newman had forfeited the high place he once held in the Roman Catholic world. The nominal grounds of this alleged forfeiture were a sermon which he had recently preached on the Temporal Power of the Pope, and some "heterodox" passages in the *Apologia*. The ungraciousness of these attacks was manifest, and their injustice was scarcely less so. Twenty years of fidelity to the cause for which he had made such enormous sacrifices and broken such affectionate ties, ought to have insured him from the petty jealousies and dis-affections of a clique. To the credit of the Roman

Catholic body, very little sympathy was shown with these attacks. On the other hand, Dr. Newman was himself the object of a very marked display of sympathy. A large number of influential Catholics met at Stafford on the 9th of April, 1867, and showed their attachment to him by adopting an address in which they expressed their deep pain at the anonymous attacks he had endured. "Any blow," they said, "that touches you, wounds the Catholic Church in this country." The numerous and important signatures appended to this address gave it a representative character. In his letter of reply Dr. Newman said, "The attacks of opponents are never hard to bear when the person who is the subject of them is conscious to himself that they are undeserved. But in the present instance I have small cause indeed for pain or regret at this occurrence, since they have at once elicited in my behalf the warm feeling of so many dear friends who know me well, and of so many others whose good opinion is the more impartial for the very reason that I am not personally known to them. Of such men, whether friends or strangers to me, I would a hundred times rather receive the generous sympathy than have escaped the misrepresentations which are the occasion of their showing it." Some years afterwards he made another public reference to the painful episode of these unjust attacks. By a deputation of Irish peers, judges, and Roman Catholic bishops, waiting upon him to congratulate him on his accession to the Cardinalate, it was remarked that he had not been altogether spared the dishonouring misrepresentations which have been the portion of the best and greatest of mankind. Dr. Newman, in acknowledging the compliment, said, "Reference has been made to the accident that in past years I have not always been understood, or had justice done to my real sentiments and intentions, in influential quarters at home and abroad. I will not deny that on several occasions this has been my trial, and I say this without assuming that I had no blame myself in its coming upon me. But I was conscious myself of a firm faith in the Catholic Church and a loyalty to the Holy See, and that I had been blessed with a fair measure of success in my work; and that prejudice and misrepresentation do not last for ever And now my wonder is, as I feel it, that the sunshine is come out so soon and with so fair a promise of lasting through my evening."

CHAPTER VII.

The Dogma of Papal Infallibility—Catholic Objections to the Definition—Dr. Newman condemns it as ill-timed—The Massacre of St. Bartholomew and Pope Gregory XIII.—Mr. Gladstone's Article on Ritualism—His Charge against Romanism—Pamphlet on the Vatican Decrees—Its Reception by Catholics—Newman's Letter to the Duke of Norfolk—The Claims of Conscience—Mr. Gladstone's Reply—The "Grammar of Assent."

In the year 1870, the dogma of Papal Infallibility received the assent of the Œcumenical Council sitting at Rome. Its effect was to give to the Pope's *ex cathedrâ* decisions the force of a *de fide* revelation, binding on the consciences and unquestioning obedience of all good Catholics. The Council further determined that, in order to speak *ex cathedrâ*, the Pope must at least speak "as exercising the office of Pastor and Doctor of all Christians, defining, by virtue of his Apostolical authority, a doctrine whether of faith or of morals for the acceptance of the universal Church." Practically the doctrine of the Pope's infallibility had been accepted and acted upon by the Roman Church for many centuries, but it had never, until then, been formulated by definition or, in the shape of a dogma, promulgated as an essential of fidelity. The faith of Roman Catholics, objectively considered, can never

change. It cannot be added to or diminished, in their
eyes, as it is simply the "deposit" of revealed truth,
committed to the guardianship of the Church, to be
announced by her to the world, under the guidance of
the Holy Spirit. The "definitions" of the Church do
not, to the Roman Catholic, make *new* faith; they only
declare certain doctrines to be "of faith" which before
(however generally believed as truths) were not *defined*
dogmas and might, therefore, be denied without sub-
jecting those who denied them to the charge of heresy.
The Apostles' Creed was the first great "definition" of
Christian Faith. The Nicene and Athanasian Creeds
were similar "definitions"; also that of Pope Pius the
Fourth. The Vatican decree, "defining" the infallibility of the Head of the Church, when speaking
ex cathedrâ on a matter of Faith or the Moral Law, was
the last "definition" of the Church. In just the same
way the doctrine of the Immaculate Conception had, in
1854, been crystallised into a dogma binding on the
consciences of the faithful. The infallibility of the
Church has ever been believed, as a fundamental truth,
by Roman Catholics of every age; because they hold
that the Holy Spirit speaks through the Church as to the
truths to be believed, and the moral law to be obeyed,
by men, in order to eternal salvation. But questions
often arose as to where this infallibility resided,
whether in the Pontiff, speaking in the fulness of his
authority as Head of the Church, or in the decisions of
General Councils duly sanctioned by him, or only when
such decisions or decrees were accepted by the great

CATHOLIC OBJECTIONS TO THE DEFINITION. 109

body of the Church throughout the world. The belief most generally held was that now defined by the Vatican Council, declaring the decree of the Roman Pontiff, when speaking *ex cathedrâ* and defining a matter of faith or moral law, to be "irreformable in itself" and binding on the whole Church.

Nevertheless the new "definition" of 1870 was not carried into effect with unanimity. More than eighty of the bishops absented themselves from the Council, and would have nothing to do with its act. Out of these formidable dissensions grew the Old Catholic movement with Dr. Döllinger at its head, who rejecting these novelties of dogma, seceded from the Church and took with them an erudition which, it was thought, could hardly be replaced. Outside the Council, the Vatican vote was received with feelings of the most contradictory kind, even among members of the Catholic Church. Some thought the Papal claims themselves too extensive; others, who were not willing to dispute the decree on this score, considered that it was ill-timed. Its practical outcome seemed to be that whatever the Pope might do was to be regarded as free from error. This, at all events, was the popular view of the dogma, although it was afterwards sought to be modified by the attenuating explanations of a subtle dialectical skill. Grave feelings and apprehensions were excited by the definition of Papal Infallibility, at a juncture when the cooler heads of the Church were loath to excite the popular clamour of her enemies. What intelligent

Protestants thought of it is within the recollection of everybody. It may be that the interpretation put upon the possible scope of the dogma was in some cases exaggerated; but the fact that many of the more influential Catholics resented it, even when limited to the domain of faith and morals, shows that the Protestant feeling on the matter could not have sprung entirely from ill-informed prejudice. Dr. Newman was one of those who had always accepted this doctrine of personal infallibility in a certain limited sense. His theory, which was that of the majority of his co-religionists in this country, was that the Pope was free from error only in his office as teacher of faith and morals, and that in his personal acts he was as liable to err as any other man. It is easy to see what a flood of casuistry might be evolved out of a differentiation so subtle. Nevertheless it satisfied men whose largeness of intellect forbids us to think that they were at all slow to perceive even the most delicate shade of its import. But the prudence of the Œcumenical definition by no means gave equal satisfaction in all quarters. Dr. Newman resented it on the ground of inexpediency. His view found expression in a letter to Bishop Ullathorne of Birmingham, which, although not intended for publication, by some means found its way into print and gave rise, temporarily, to an impression that the doctrine itself failed to meet with his acceptance.

"Rome ought," he said, "to be a name to lighten

the heart at all times, and a Council's proper office
is, when some great heresy or other evil impends,
to inspire hope and confidence in the faithful; but
now we have the greatest meeting which ever has
been seen, and that at Rome, infusing into us by
the accredited organs of Rome and of its partisans
(such as the *Civilta*, the *Armonia*, the *Univers*,
and the *Tablet*) little else than fear and dismay.
When we are all at rest, and have no doubts, and
—at least practically, not to say doctrinally—hold
the Holy Father to be infallible, suddenly there is
thunder in the clear sky, and we are told to
prepare for something, we know not what, to try
our faith, we know not how. No impending danger
is to be averted, but a great difficulty is to be
created. Is this the proper work of an Œcumenical
Council ?

"As to myself personally, please God, I do not
expect any trial at all; but I cannot help suffering
with the many souls who are suffering, and I look
with anxiety at the prospect of having to defend
decisions which may not be difficult to my own private
judgment, but may be most difficult to maintain
logically in the face of historical facts.

"What have we done to be treated as the faithful
never were treated before ? When has a definition
de fide been a luxury of devotion and not a stern
painful necessity ? Why should an aggressive insolent
faction be allowed 'to make the heart of the just sad,
whom the Lord hath not made sorrowful ?' Why

cannot we be let alone, when we have pursued peace and thought no evil ?

"I assure you, my Lord, some of the truest minds are driven one way and another, and do not know where to rest their feet,—one day determining 'to give up all theology as a bad job,' and recklessly to believe henceforth almost that the Pope is impeccable ; at another, tempted to 'believe all the worst which a book like Janus says;' others 'doubting about the capacity possessed by Bishops drawn from all corners of the earth to judge what is fitting for European society,' and then, again, angry with the Holy See for listening to the 'flattery of a clique of Jesuits, Redemptorists, and converts.'

"Then, again, think of the store of Pontifical scandals in the history of eighteen centuries which have partly been poured forth and partly are still to come. What Murphy inflicted upon us in one way M. de Veuillot is indirectly bringing on us in another. And then, again, the blight which is following upon the multitude of Anglican Ritualists, &c., who themselves perhaps,—at least their leaders,—may never become Catholics, but who are leavening the various English denominations and parties (far beyond their own range) with principles and sentiments tending towards their ultimate absorption into the Catholic Church.

"With these thoughts ever before me, I am continually asking myself whether I ought not to make my feelings public, but all I do is to pray those early doctors of the Church whose intercession would decide the matter—(Augustine, Ambrose, and Jerome, Athanasius, Chrysostom, and Basil)—to avert the great calamity.

"If it is God's will that the Pope's infallibility is defined, then is it God's will to throw back 'the times and moments' of that triumph which he has destined for His kingdom, and I shall feel I have but to bow my head to His adorable, inscrutable Providence."

The unauthorised publication of this letter made a considerable stir in the religious world, and Dr. Newman incurred the censure of the more "thorough" of the Catholic hierarchy. The Pope himself was understood to be grieved that such a document should have found its way into print. The authority of the writer, although he held no high rank in the priesthood, lent a special importance to the burning words of his protest. Its implied assent to the doctrine of the Pope's personal infallibility scarcely lessened the tremendous force of the rebuke administered to the inexpediency of the Council's action. By some of his critics, indeed, Dr. Newman was accused of having denied the doctrine of Papal Infallibility. There was no warrant for this imputation, but it was so persistently repeated that at length he felt called upon to declare in express terms that he had never for a moment questioned the doctrine. In a letter to Mr. Capes, referring to the attack of a nameless critic, he says, "He assumes that I did not hold or profess the doctrine of the Pope's Infallibility till the time of the Vatican Council, whereas I have committed myself

I

to it in print again and again from 1845 to 1867. And, on the other hand, as it so happens—though I held it, as I have ever done—I have had no occasion to profess it, whether in print or otherwise, since that date. Anyone who knows my writings will recollect that in saying so I state a simple fact." It would scarcely profit us to follow in detail the controversy which ensued, especially as it was to take a more important shape later on. The grumblings of the defenders of the dogma gradually wore themselves out. By-and-bye, such is the irony of fate, Dr. Newman was called upon by the common consent of his people to answer the more serious of the indictments brought against the Vatican decrees by those who saw in them a potentiality for bringing about civil confusion and a divided allegiance.

Prior, however, to the notable controversy with Mr. Gladstone, there was a sharp and instructive discussion in the public papers arising out of the application of the dogma of Infallibility to the Massacre of St. Bartholomew. Pope Gregory XIII.'s connection with this bloody episode is not, perhaps, based upon the clearest historical evidence, but there is some evidence to support the theory that he gave his consent, with all the authority it implied, to the authors of the massacre. At all events, he ordered a medal to be struck in commemoration of the event. Everyone admits, nowadays, that the massacre was a crime of the deepest dye, and the critics of Romanism and of its new pretensions, in 1872, put the pertinent question, whether an act iniquitous in itself was to be regarded as the infallible work of the inspired Vicar of God? In September of that year the Times had an article on the subject, which drew from Dr. Newman the following reply :—" You have lately in your article on the 'Massacre of St. Bartholomew' thrown down a challenge to us on a most serious subject. I have no claim to speak for my brethren; but I speak in default of better men. No Pope can make evil good. No Pope has any power over those eternal moral principles which God has imprinted on our hearts and consciences. If any Pope has, with his eyes open, approved treachery and cruelty, let those defend that Pope who can. If any Pope, at any time, has had his mind so occupied with the desirableness of the Church's triumph over her enemies as to be dead to the treacherous and savage acts by which that triumph was achieved, let those who feel disposed say that in such conduct he acted up to his high office of maintaining justice and showing mercy. Craft and cruelty, and whatever is base and wicked, have a sure Nemesis, and eventually strike the heads of those who are guilty of them. Whether in matter of fact Pope Gregory XIII. had a share in the guilt of the St. Bartholomew Massacre, must be proved to me before I believe it. It is commonly said, in his defence, that he had an untrue one-sided account of the matter presented to him, and acted upon misinformation. This involves a question of fact which historians must decide. But even if they decide against the Pope, his Infallibility is in no respect compromised. Infallibility is not Impeccability. Even Caiaphas prophesied, and Gregory XIII. was not quite a Caiaphas."

These minor controversies, however, paled by the side of that which presently ensued. The bearing of the Vatican Decrees was considered by many eminent Protestants to be hostile to the individual freedom of Roman Catholics in England. They understood those decrees to be capable of a political construction. If the Pope's voice was binding as an obligatory matter of conscience in questions of faith and morals, there was no knowing what affairs of politics and state might not be included in the domain of faith and morals. The Pope, they argued, really set up a paramount authority which Catholics were bound to obey, even though, in doing so, they gave up their allegiance to the lawful sovereign. The members of the Roman Catholic Church, on the other hand, said that the Pope's infallibility bore upon the domain of thought, not of action, and that his prerogative lay in speculative matters, not in laws, commands, or measures. It was denied—emphatically and indignantly denied— that Romanists were a whit less loyal than their Protestant neighbours. Mr. Gladstone, in the recess of 1874, gave a fillip to controversial activity by a passage in an article on "Ritualism" in the pages of the *Contemporary Review*. "At no time," he said, "since the sanguinary reign of Mary has such a scheme"—*i.c.*, an effort on the part of a handful of the clergy to Romanise the Church and people of England—"been possible. But, if it had been possible in the seventeenth or eighteenth century, it would still have become impossible in the nineteenth; when Rome has substituted for the proud boast of *Semper Eadem* a policy of violence and change in faith; when she has refurbished and paraded anew every rusty tool she was fondly thought to have disused; when no one can become her convert without renouncing his moral and mental freedom, and placing his civil loyalty and duty at the mercy of another; and when she has equally repudiated modern thought and ancient history." This passage in Mr. Gladstone's paper excited the indignation of his Roman Catholic fellow-subjects in an extraordinary degree. It seemed as if they had forgotten all at once the part he had taken in removing the disabilities under which they had so long laboured, and especially his great act of statesmanship in putting an end to the dominance of the Established Church in Ireland. He was fiercely and even bitterly assailed, so much so that he felt an elaborate justification of his words to be necessary. This appeared in a pamphlet on *The Vatican Decrees — in their Bearing on Civil Allegiance; a Political Expostulation.* He divided his case into four propositions, embracing the several charges of the passage in the *Contemporary Review.* Of these the third, namely, that "no one can now become the convert of Rome without renouncing his moral and mental freedom, and placing his civil loyalty and duty at the mercy of another," was the most important. After a minute analysis of the doctrine of Papal Infallibility, Mr. Gladstone summarised the effects of the dogma by stating that absolute obedience had been declared to be due to the Pope, at the peril of salvation, not alone in faith and in morals, but in all things which concern the discipline and government of the Church. "Thus," he continued, "are swept into the Papal net whole multitudes of facts, whole systems of government, prevailing, though in different degrees, in every country in the world. Even in the United States, where the severance between Church and State is supposed to be complete, a long catalogue might be drawn up of subjects belonging to the domain and competency of the State, but also undeniably affecting the government of the Church; such as, by way of example, marriage, burial, education, prison discipline, blasphemy, poor relief, incorporation, workmen's religious endowments, vows of celibacy and obedience. In Europe the circle is far wider, the points of contact and of interlacing almost innumerable. But on all matters respecting which any Pope may think proper to declare that they concern either faith, or morals, or the government or discipline of the Church, he claims, with the approval of a Council, undoubtedly Œcumenical in the Roman sense, the absolute obedience, at the peril of salvation, of every member of his communion. . . . It is well to remember that this claim . . .

is lodged in open day by, and in the reign of, a Pontiff who has condemned free speech, free writing, a free press, toleration of Nonconformity, liberty of conscience, the study of civil and philosophical matters in independence of the ecclesiastical authority, marriage unless sacramentally contracted, and the definition by the State of the civil rights of the Church; who has demanded from the Church, therefore, the title to define its own civil rights, together with a divine right to civil immunities, and a right to use physical force; and who has also proudly asserted that the Popes of the middle ages with their Councils did not invade the rights of princes."

Mr. Gladstone deduced from his arguments the conclusion that the Pope claimed from every convert and member of his Church that he shall "place his loyalty and civil duty at the mercy of another," that other being his Holiness. Having dealt with the propositions, the essayist proceeded to discuss the questions whether, being true, they were material, and whether being true and material, they were proper to be set forth by him. With regard to the latter, he pointed out that notwithstanding what the Liberal party had done for Roman Catholics in the past, the rejection of the Irish University Bill was due to the influence of the Roman Catholic prelacy of Ireland. If this were the place to show it, it might be proved that the inherent defects of the measure, and its unsatisfactoriness to Liberal feeling, were as much the cause of its failure as the opposition of the Irish Bishops, who, whether they were instigated thereto by Rome or not, had an unquestionable right to use their influence against a measure which, in their opinion, fell short of the just claims of their creed. This, however, is quite by the way. The pamphlet was undoubtedly an able and lucid exposition of the popular view, and to the large majority of Englishmen who read it, it must have carried conviction, at any rate as regarded its main thesis. In a few weeks a hundred and twenty thousand copies were sold. Many Roman Catholics of eminence, lay as well as clerical, replied to it. A great divergence of view was made manifest. It became more evident than ever that the Vatican Decrees did not meet with the full acceptance of many distinguished Catholic families in England. Lord Camoys, Lord Acton, and Mr. Henry Petre declared their agreement, more or less, with Mr. Gladstone's views. But most of the replies were of an antagonistic rather than of a sympathetic character. The Ultramontane press was, naturally, in its severest mood. No more noteworthy answer was forthcoming, however, than the temperate and closely-reasoned reply made by Dr. Newman. This took the form of a letter to the Duke of Norfolk, and it was published in pamphlet form very early in 1875. It would be idle to deny that Dr. Newman made out a strong case. So skilful a controversialist could scarcely have failed to present a plausible, and even an effective answer. The drift of his argument was, in effect, to minimize the nature of the Papal claims, and to show that there was no danger of their being exerted to the detriment of Catholic loyalty. It became necessary for Dr. Newman, as he proceeded with his argument, to refer to the letter of 1870, already quoted, and to various rumours that had been circulated. Mr. Gladstone, in alluding to this letter n his pamphlet, had spoken of it as "remarkable," and as "a censure by the first living theologian now within the Roman Communion." Dr. Newman, after denying that there was a particle of truth in the statement that he was at one time on the point of uniting with Dr. Döllinger and his party, said: ' They [such reports] arise from forgetfulness on the part of those who spread them that there are two sides of ecclesiastical acts, that right ends are often prosecuted by very unworthy means, and that in consequence those who like myself oppose a mode of action, are not necessarily opposed to the issue for which it has been adopted." Referring to the publication of his private letter, he said: "It was one of the most confidential I ever wrote in my life. I wrote it to my own Bishop, under a deep sense of the responsibility I should incur, were I not to speak out to him my own mind. I put the matter from me when I had said my say, and kept no proper copy of the letter. To my dismay I saw it in the public prints—to this day I do not know, nor suspect, how it got there. I cannot withdraw it, for I never put it forward, so it will remain in the columns of the newspapers whether I will or not; but I withdraw it as far as I can, by declaring that it was never meant for the public eye."

It would be impracticable to give here anything like a sufficient summary of the arguments adduced by Dr. Newman in his contention with Mr. Gladstone, although one or two of them may be alluded to. That those arguments, admirably arranged and expressed though they were, fell short of convincing Protestant readers may, perhaps, be taken for granted. Dr. Newman's object was to narrow the field, and to show that the claims of the Pope were not meant to extend into the domain of practical politics. In doing so he took a learned and comprehensive survey of the whole question. One scarcely knows whether to admire more the enormous range of his theological reading, or his delightful lucidity of expression, or the masterly way in which he marshalled his arguments. He said that the cases were extreme and highly improbable in which he should obey the Pope and not the State. "The circumference of State jurisdiction and of Papal are for the most part quite apart from each other; there are just some few degrees out of the 360 in which they intersect, and Mr. Gladstone, instead of letting these cases of inter-section alone, till they actually occur, asks me what I should do if I found myself placed in the space intersected. If I must answer then, I should say distinctly that did the State tell me in a question of worship to do what the Pope told me not to do, I should obey the Pope, and should think it no sin, if I used all the power and the influence I possessed as a citizen to prevent such a bill passing the Legislature, and to effect its repeal if it did." In like manner there were hypothetical though remotely improbable cases in which he might find it his duty to obey the State and disobey the Pope. He gave an "absolute obedience" neither to Pope nor Queen. If one of these far-fetched conflicts of authority should arise, and he failed to get guidance in the quarters where he looked for it, he should decide the case for himself on its own merits. That is to say, he would resort to private judgment in extraordinary and rare emergencies, if they could be regarded as coming within the range of possibility. So, too, in matters of conscience. Conscience, in its true meaning, was of higher authority than a Papal command, and should receive obedience if by any chance the two happened to clash. "Certainly," said Dr. Newman, by way of clenching this part of his argument, "if I am obliged to bring religion into after-dinner toasts (which, indeed, does not seem quite the thing), I shall drink,—to the Pope, if you please,—still, to Conscience first, and to the Pope afterwards." Referring to Mr. Gladstone's statement that the Holy See had condemned the liberty of the press, of conscience, and of worship, the reverend Father construed it to mean that liberty of conscience and worship was the *inherent right* of all men, that it ought to be proclaimed in *every* rightly-constituted society, that it was a right to *all sorts of liberty*, such that it ought not to be restrained by any authority, ecclesiastical *or civil*, as far as public speaking, printing, or any other public manifestation of opinions is concerned. In other words, it was the liberty of *every* one to give *public* utterance, in *every* possible shape, by *every* possible channel, without *any* let or hindrance from God or man, to *all* his notions *whatsoever*. All that the Pope had done was to deny a universal,—a universal liberty to all men to say out whatever doctrines they may hold, by preaching or the press, uncurbed by the Church or civil power. Dr. Newman next proceeded to explain away the importance of the Syllabus, which was, he said, a mere index to propositions which during many years had been condemned by Pope Pius IX. in formal Allocutions, and carried in itself no weight. Not the least interesting part of the Letter was the reasoning by which he convinced himself that notwithstanding the withdrawal of no fewer than eighty Bishops from the Council, when the dogma was adopted, it still had all the weight and authority which would have belonged to a unanimous acceptance. The concluding divisions were devoted to a general diminution of the force of the dogma and a limitation of its sphere of operations.

Mr. Gladstone had, of course, dealt with that interpretation of the dogma which appeared to bear out his own convictions. In a reply, written a month

or two later, he pronounced Dr. Newman's Letter
to the Duke of Norfolk to be of the highest interest
as a psychological study. "Whatever he writes,
whether we agree with him or not, presents to us
this great attraction as well as advantage, that we
have everywhere the man in his work, that the
words are the transparent covering of his nature.
If there be obliquity in them, it is purely intellectual obliquity; the work of an intellect sharp
enough to cut the diamond, and bright as the
diamond which it cuts. How rarely it is found, in
the wayward and inscrutable records of our race,
that with these instruments of an almost superhuman
force and subtlety, robustness of character and energy
of will are or can be developed in the same extraordinary proportions, so as to integrate that structure
of combined thought and action which makes life
a moral whole." With this generous estimate of a
controversial adversary—an estimate in all ways
characteristic of Mr. Gladstone's chivalrous nature—
very few impartial critics will disagree. The upshot
of the discussion, if it can be said to have had any
upshot at all, was that the loyalty of the Queen's
Roman Catholic subjects remained untainted and
secure, while the honours of the chief disputants may
be said to have been divided. The victory lies with
him with whom we are most in sympathy. It is
according to the bias of the reader that judgment
will be given, and in a matter so intimately bound
up with religious bias as that of the Vatican Decrees

it would be impossible to say that either of the champions had completely and signally worsted his foe.

In the same year was published that remarkable work of Christian apologetics, *The Grammar of Assent.* In this skilfully argued work Dr. Newman has vindicated the claims of the Christian religion upon human belief. He deals in it with the inner evidences of belief, and with the processes which lead the mind to assent to them, and his object is to free those processes from the yoke of formal and technical logic. It is a work which Protestants as well as Catholics, with few exceptions, can unreservedly admire, inasmuch as its motive is not a defence of Catholicism in particular, but of Christianity.

CHAPTER VIII.

No official recognition of the service rendered by Dr. Newman followed his Letter to the Duke of Norfolk. Others who had contributed to the discussion, and whose vindication of the Vatican Decrees had been more thorough, were rewarded with titular distinctions and ecclesiastical rank. Archbishop Manning was made a Cardinal. Apostolical favours in the shape of Approbations and Benedictions were showered upon those who had upheld the construction of the Papal Acts most in accordance with the views of the Roman Curia. Neither Missive nor Benediction, however, was sent to Dr. Newman. He remained a plain Oratorian Father, and while one of the two prominent divines who had defended the Decrees received a signal mark of the Pope's approval, the other, and the more eminent, was treated with what his countrymen could not help regarding as a sullen neglect. Honours, however, were forthcoming from a different source, animated

by a generous recognition of his unsurpassed
intellectual qualities, apart from the doctrines
they were employed to support. Towards the close
of 1877 he was elected an Honorary Fellow
of Trinity College, Oxford. This was a signal
mark of honour. Trinity had been his first college. It
was endeared to him by many pleasant associations,
and the ties of warm and never-to-be-forgotten friendships. "Trinity," he says in the *Apologia*, "had
never been unkind to me." Hence this mark of
recognition was one of special acceptability. There
was an added graciousness in it due to the conditions
of his faith. A few years earlier, before the abolition
of University tests, such an honour would have been
impossible. The idea of a distinguished Roman
Catholic being selected for one of the high posts
in Oxford would have been too much for the old
intolerant days of Church of England prerogative. Dr.
Newman's religious professions being no longer a
"disability," nothing could have been more fitting
than the distinction conferred upon him by his old
college. Nor did the college itself fail to gain by the
distinction it bestowed. The lustre of a great name
was reflected upon its own reputation. It became
forthwith identified with one of the profoundest
scholars and most eminent men of the age, in a
far more distinct way than by having been the home
of his undergraduate days. And it became the means
of what in one sense may almost be called a
reconciliation between Dr. Newman and Oxford itself.

When he quitted Littlemore in 1846, and left behind him the towers and spires of Oxford, it was with the idea that his association with the University was broken for ever. He did not expect ever to have any identity with, or practical interest in it again. He had seen the spires from the railway, but Oxford itself he had never revisited. The Trinity fellowship was the means of his renewing the connection by once more setting foot amid the familiar scenes of thirty-two years before. At the latter end of February, 1878, Dr. Newman revisited Oxford. He was the guest of the Rev. S. Wayte, President of Trinity College. He met a number of his old friends at dinner, and on the following day paid a long visit to Dr. Pusey, at Christ Church. What a flood of recollections,—what a host of surmises,—such a meeting must have called up. These two distinguished men were, at one time, on the same road and seemingly travelling towards the same goal. Both fell under the rebuke of the authorities. Dr. Newman had been censured, in effect, for the views enunciated in Tract XC. Dr. Pusey had been suspended from his preachership not long afterwards for a sermon on the Eucharist. One went over to Rome; the other remained in the Anglican Communion to be the apostle of "high" doctrine, and to give a name to that school of "Romanisers" which has since been merged in the Ritualist movement. Tomes of controversy might be said to have been represented in the conjunction

K

of these two eminent theologians, each representative
of, and well able to champion, his particular cause.
During his visit to Oxford, Dr. Newman spent some
time at Keble College, in which he was naturally
much interested, and on one of the days he dined at
Trinity Hall, at the high table, in his academical dress.
Two years and three months later, that is in May, 1880,
he again visited Oxford, met a distinguished company
at a conversazione in the College Garden, and preached
at the Roman Catholic Chapel in St. Giles's.

In 1877, Dr. Newman published a collected edition
of his numerous works. No pretence has been made
in this sketch to chronicle, even by name, the whole
of his contributions to religious literature. Nor is
it necessary to repair the omission by a mere
lifeless record of their titles. Reference may,
however, be made to the *Miscellaneous and Critical
Essays*, which have been widely read and admired;
and to *Calista : a Sketch of the Third Century*, a
touching story of a beautiful Greek girl, who becomes
a convert to Christianity after a fierce struggle
between human affection and religious faith. The
characters in this work are finely drawn, and
vividly contrasted, and the whole surroundings of
the period are caught with admirable fidelity. In
the re-issue of his works referred to Dr. Newman
included his pre-Catholic writings, annotating them
where he felt that the views needed refutation, or
the mis-statements rectifying. An interesting contribution to his autobiography is furnished in the

Preface. "It stands to reason, he says, "that these volumes must contain various statements, which I am sorry to have made, and which I reproduce at the present time not without pain. Gladly would I obliterate them, but that cannot be; and I have only the alternative of publishing them afresh with what I consider a refutation, or leaving them unanswered, to the chance of publication by others at some future time. I have chosen to re-publish them myself, and perhaps it would be want of faith in the Truth, or some over appreciation of my own controversial powers, if I had any dread lest my present explanations in behalf of the Catholic Religion could be inferior in cogency to the charges which I once brought against it.

"As I said in 1871, in the advertisement to my essays, 'The author cannot destroy what he has once put into print: *Litera scripta manet*. He might suppress it for a time; but sooner or later his power over it will cease. And then, if it is either in its matter or its drift adapted to benefit the cause which it was intended to support, at the time when it was given to the world, it will be re-published in spite of his later disavowal of it. In order to anticipate the chance of its being thus used after his death, the only way open to him is while living, to show why it has ceased to approve itself to his own judgment. If he does as much as this, he may reasonably hope that either no reprint of it will be made hereafter, or that the reprint of his first thoughts will in fairness be allowed to carry with it a reprint of his second. Moreover, he is sanguine that he has been able to reduce what is un-Catholic in these volumes, whether in argument or in statement, to the position of those 'Differentates' which figure in dogmatic treatises of theology, and which are elaborately drawn out and set forth to best advantage, in order that they may be the more carefully and satisfactorily answered.' "

These were the most noteworthy public events of Dr. Newman's life, in the years just prior to his elevation to the Cardinalate. He was now an old man, and for him the heat and confusion of controversy were past. In his reply to Mr. Gladstone he said those utterances were likely to be his " last words," and so, in one sense, they were. The soldier had fought zealously, and now he was not loath to put up his sword, and leave the strife to younger and lustier men. But his life was still one of activity, of routine duties consistently performed, of unremitting study, of ceaseless vigilance in his pious offices. A pleasant writer in the *World* has given such a complete sketch of Dr. Newman's habits about this time that some passages of it are worth quoting: —" As Dr. Newman's days grow fewer, they grow longer. He has ever been an early riser, and now from five in the morning until an unknown hour at night he is busily engaged in redeeming the time. His first two hours are given to devotion. Shortly after seven he says his mass—usually for some years past in the chapel of the Bona Mors—in which the souls of the founders and Catholic benefactors of his old colleges at Oxford are always remembered. At about eight o'clock he appears in the refectory, where he breakfasts in silence, after the custom of religious houses, attacking meanwhile the pile of correspondence which awaits him on the table. Then his own room receives him, and until half-past two or three in the afternoon correspondence, study, and the duties involved in the government of the house and school engross him. An hour or two in the afternoon is given to exercise, for he is still a great pedestrian; the community dinner is at six o'clock, and on days when his turn comes round 'the Father' girds on the apron of service, and waits upon his brethren, not himself sitting down until they are served. All eat in silence, only broken by the voice of the Lector, who from the pulpit in the corner reads first a chapter from the Vulgate, then a chapter of the life of a saint, and lastly, a portion from some modern work of general interest. When dinner is over, questions in some department of theological science are proposed by him whose turn it is. Each in succession gives his opinion, ending with the usual formula, 'But I speak under correction.' Then the proposer sums up, and the Fathers adjourn to a neighbouring parlour, where coffee is served and the pent-up flood of conversation bursts forth—the play of wit and fancy, the wealth of anecdote and reminiscence, the tender glances at the past, the keen remarks on the public events of the day, the shrewd practical observations on their own domestic and personal concerns. In all of which the Superior fully bears his part, as much at home here as among his graver pursuits, his clear musical voice interposing frequently to add the contribution of his *mitis sapientia* to the genial hour, which recalls to one the description given of the first Oratory over which St. Philip Neri himself presided, 'the school of Christian mirth.' Perhaps the two things which most strike the visitor among these ecclesiastics are their thoroughly English tone, and the liberality, in the highest sense, of their views. So passes Dr. Newman's life in his Birmingham home, its tranquil course broken at rare intervals by visits to old and cherished friends, chiefly of his Oxford days, or by retirement to a tiny country house of the Oratorians, a few miles distant, at Rednal, round which is the little churchyard where they are buried. It is a pretty little spot, well away from the smoke and din of Birmingham; and here Dr. Newman will sometimes spend days in absolute seclusion, whether seeking rest from pro-longed labour or unbroken time for more assiduous toil. It was here that the most closely reasoned of his works, the *Grammar of Assent*, was composed; but the books with which the walls are lined bear evidence that lighter literature is not disregarded. Miss Austen, Thackeray, Anthony Trollope, Sir

Walter Scott, Mrs. Gaskell, are favourite authors with the great theologian. Of modern English poets, Wordsworth, Southey, and Crabbe are highly valued by him, and are constantly read. Music, again, has ever been a solace to him, and has been lovingly cultivated. Most educated men know the passage in the Oxford *University Sermons* in which 'the mysterious stirrings of heart, and keen emotions and strange yearnings after we know not what, and awful impressions we know not whence,' produced in us by the great masters of musical sound, are described in words of majestic eloquence which it would be hard to parallel. As might have been expected, the man who could write thus of music is himself no mean musician. A story is told—we know not with what truth—that on one occasion a Protestant Boanerges visiting Birmingham sent a pompous invitation to the great convert to dispute publicly with him in the Town Hall, to which Dr. Newman replied that he had small skill in controversy, and must decline to enter the lists with so redoubtable a champion; but that his friends credited him with some power of playing the violin, and that he would be happy to meet his challenger at a trial of strength on that instrument."

This seems a convenient place for enumerating one or two of Dr. Newman's more conspicuous traits. His method of life, for years, has been of the very simplest. Those who have been privileged to visit him in his own little room at the Oratory have been struck by the comparative bareness of its furniture. His bed, hung all round with curtains, stands screened off in one corner; a little square of carpet occupies the middle of the apartment; there are no evidences of luxury save those afforded by the presence of books; simplicity prevails on every hand. It is characteristic of this distinguished man that he cares nothing for the treasures of this world. His life has been one of severe self-discipline. It would have been no difficult matter for him to have surrounded himself with the material evidences of refinement, and some, at least, of the purchasable comforts which, in the ideas of most men, go so far in contributing to mundane contentment. There is nothing of the kind, however, in the surroundings of Dr. Newman's home life. He loves, and has always loved, plain and homely ways, retirement from the busy haunts of men, the pleasures of contemplation, and the rich delights of a scholar's occupation. In the unique library of theology possessed by the Oratory he finds society and counsellors. Nor has age caused his diligence to wane. In these latter years, when the allotted span has long run by, he has got through more work than many a fairly industrious man in the prime of life. Up till quite recently—I believe up to the present time—he has assisted at the monthly examination of the more advanced boys at the Oratory School. A year or two ago he found time from the more serious duties of his position to revise Terence's licentious but witty comedy

Eunuchus, and to make it acceptable for presentation by the pupils without sacrificing any of its diverting quality; and last summer he effected an equally decorous transformation in the case of the *Phormio*; performing the task of purgation with an ingenuity and taste worthy of his reputation as a finished classical scholar. The interest of the latter of these presentations was increased by the fact that he wrote for it a prologue in terse and elegant Latin, and in equally pithy and pointed English as well. The English version may be quoted as a specimen of his scholarly recreations at the ripe age of fourscore:—

> " What Attic Terence wrote of old for Rome,
> We, in our Northern accents, lisp to-night;
> What heathen Terence spoke to heathen ears,
> We speak with Christian tongues to Christian men :
> Doing the while this service to the Bard,
> That the rare beauty of his classic wit
> We by our pruning make more beautiful.
>
> O happy art, which Terence never knew,
> But they have learned, who aim in everything
> To choose the good, and pass the evil by !
> These, as they pace the tangled path of life,
> Cleanse from this earth its earthly dross away,
> And clothe it with a pure supernal light.
>
> Neighbours and friends, what I have more to say—
> It is not much—concerns our actors here,
> Fresh, tender souls, and palpitating hearts,
> Boys, who, though boys, essay the parts of men,
> And are the first within this Catholic fold
> To represent a classic comedy.
> Be kind—they strive with no inglorious aim ;
> Where they do well, applaud ; and if in aught
> They shall come short, be mild and merciful.
>
> Prologue enough ; let Davus enter now,
> And lend his ear, while Geta tells his tale."

All who have been present at these occasional performances by the Oratory boys will recall the Doctor's quiet enjoyment of the acting, and the simple, unostentatious manner in which he has entered into the humours of the Latin comedians. His kindness, indeed, has always been notable. Not long ago a clergyman of the Church of England with whom he had formerly had an epistolary controversy, happened to be in Birmingham, and took occasion to call upon him. He was greeted with the most graceful of welcomes, and spent, as he told a friend, one of the most delightful hours of his life. Dr. Newman has the rare faculty of making everyone with whom he comes in contact feel the influence of his sweetness and geniality of disposition. It has often happened that the children of the Birmingham Catholic Schools have obtained leave to spend a day at Rednal, near to which the Fathers of the Oratory own a few acres of heather-covered hill on the Bromsgrove Lickey range. In the bracing air of this picturesque seclusion the youngsters enjoy themselves thoroughly. On one occasion—it was in 1874—one of the schools had this privilege while Dr. Newman, according to his wont, was seeking repose at Rednal from the monotonous and wearing cares of the Oratory. So delighted was he to have the opportunity of ministering to the happiness of these little children, —the sons and daughters, most of them, of poor people,—that he went out to meet them, conducted them through the little chapel and house, the pleasure ground, over the mountain side and on to its very top, his face beaming with joy, and his manner as complaisant as if he had been showing the attention to the children of nobles.

Dr. Newman has always taken a singular interest in young people, and has striven to add to the happiness of those, whether pupils or otherwise, with whom he has come in contact. This has been to some extent the natural outcome of an exceedingly amiable disposition. In no man of conspicuous mark in the world of thought has the combination of "sweetness and light" been more strikingly exhibited. He recalls in all things his own definition of a gentleman, which, while it reflects the gentleness and consideration for others which characterise his own conduct, is such an excellent example of his grace of literary expression, that some of its sentences are worth embodying here :—"The true gentleman carefully avoids whatever may cause a jar or a jolt in the minds of those with whom he is cast; all clashing of opinion, or collision of feeling, all restraint, or suspicion, or gloom, or resentment; his great concern being to make everyone at their ease and at home. He has his eyes on all his company; he is tender towards the bashful, gentle towards the distant, and merciful towards the absurd; he can recollect to whom he is speaking; he guards against unseasonable allusions or topics which may irritate; he is seldom prominent in conversation, and never wearisome. He makes light of favours while he does them, and seems to be receiving when he is

conferring. He never speaks of himself except when
compelled, never defends himself by a mere retort;
he has no ears for slander or gossip, is scrupulous in
imputing motives to those who interfere with him,
and interprets everything for the best. He is never
mean or little in his disputes, never takes unfair
advantage, never mistakes personalities or sharp
sayings for arguments, or insinuates evil which he
dare not say out. From a long-sighted prudence, he
observes the maxim of the ancient sage, that we
should ever conduct ourselves towards our enemy
as if he were one day to be our friend. He has
too much sense to be affronted at insults, he is too
well employed to remember injuries, and too indolent
to bear malice. He is patient, forbearing, and
resigned, on philosophical principles; he submits to
pain because it is inevitable, to bereavement because
it is irreparable, and to death because it is destiny.
If he engage in controversy of any kind, his disciplined
intellect preserves him from the blundering discourtesy
of better, perhaps, but less educated minds, who, like
blunt weapons, tear and hack instead of cutting clean,
who mistake the point in argument, waste their
strength on trifles, misconceive their adversary, and
leave the question more involved than they find it."
["*Idea of a University.*"]

CHAPTER IX.

IN the early part of 1879, rumours were afloat to the
effect that Pope Leo XIII. was desirous of conferring
some signal mark of favour upon Dr. Newman. It
was also rumoured that the distinguished Oratorian
was anxious to preserve his untitled position, and
to continue devoting himself to the studious and
educational work with which his life had been so
long identified. Of Dr. Newman it might be truly
said that he was not one of those

> " Who stoop, or lie in wait
> For wealth, for honours, or for worldly state."

In harmony with St. Philip Neri's precept he " loved
to be alone." It was therefore somewhat of a surprise
when the definite announcement was made that he
was to be raised to the Cardinalate. Nor is there
much reason to doubt that he was at first reluctant
to accept the princely position, with its attendant
dignity and responsibilities. His scruples were,

however, overcome. His Holiness treated him with
all the delicate consideration due to his venerable
age and commanding influence, but pressed the offer
on his acceptance. This pressure, from so authoritative
a source, partook of the nature of a command; and
Dr. Newman, whatever his private inclinations may
have been,—and there is no doubt that he would
have preferred to remain as he was, plain "Father
Newman," and to have pursued, apart from the
garish light which floods a great dignity, the even
tenour of his contemplative way,—felt it his duty
to obey. The names of the other eminent personages
whom the Pope selected for elevation to the Sacred
College showed clearly enough that Leo XIII. was
not bound by the Vatican traditions. Some of them
had incurred the displeasure of Pius IX. Possibly
if they had not been the nominees of one whose will
was law, the members of the College would have
exercised a veto upon more than one of them.
Newman himself can scarcely be said to have been
an acceptable colleague to some of the Ultramontane
section. The choice, however, was popular in
England. Protestants as well as Catholics felt that
tardy justice had at length been done to the ablest
and most notable of Rome's champions. The honour,
if it were really a recompense for service rendered,
ought to have come long before. It came to him
now in the fulness of years,—almost when his life's
work might be considered done, when his body had
not the strength nor his mind the disposition for the

burdens of rank. His co-religionists expressed their pleasure in terms of warm congratulation. Men of the Reformed faith, who knew what prospects he had given up for conscience sake when he quitted the Anglican Communion, were not sorry that Rome had recognised his super-eminent qualities at last. Addresses soon began to be showered upon him from various Catholic quarters. The Provost and Canons of the Chapter of Westminster were among the earliest to express their gratification. The Provost and Chapter of St. Chad's, Birmingham, gave utterance to similar feelings. The Irish Catholic members of Parliament caught up and echoed the strain. Resolutions of satisfaction were passed by the Catholic Union. To most, if not all, of these congratulations, Dr. Newman made suitable replies. To the St. Chad's Chapter he avowed that never was a man supported and sustained more generously and affectionately than he had been in time of need; and that now, when his course was nearly run, the subscribers to the address ended as they had begun some thirty years ago; bringing up before him the memories of the past, and renewing his gratitude for old and recent acts of friendliness. In replying to the Westminster address he said: "It is indeed a happiness as great as it is rare that those feelings which are commonly aroused in a man's friends after his death should, in my own case, find expression in my behalf while I am yet alive." Speaking to the Irish Catholic M.P.'s, he said: "You are the representatives of an ancient and faithful Catholic people for whom I have a deep affection," and added that no other country in the world would have treated him so graciously as theirs had done during his seven years' residence among them. All these testimonies of affection and respect must have convinced Dr. Newman that among his own people he was deeply beloved. Their spontaneity was as marked as their earnestness; their genuineness was as manifest as their loyalty. Somebody circulated a rumour about this time to the effect that Dr. Pusey had urged Dr. Newman to refuse the Cardinalate. The subject is worth referring to on account of a characteristic letter which Pusey wrote in answer to an inquiry on the subject. "The idea," he says, "of my having written to dear Newman most earnestly to refuse the Cardinalate is, of course, simply absurd. I heard at one and the same time that it had been offered to him, and that he had declined it. This was said, as far as I know, without the slightest contradiction. All the papers were full of it. I waited for a week, and then, supposing it to be certain that he had declined it, I wrote to congratulate him on the mark of confidence which the offer implied, and on his non-acceptance of the offer. It has been to me and to several of his old friends, like those old lines—'I have been honoured and obeyed, &c.' I do not know whether you love those old lines in the *Lyra Apostolica* as we do. His still life in the Oratory at Birmingham has been an ideal to me which I love to dwell upon. However, I found that people were mistaken, and that dear Newman thought that it would have been ungrateful in him towards those who had been at the pains to obtain this honour for him, and that he had accepted it, though he himself preferred obscurity. So I wrote to retract what I had said. Why do people gossip about such a sacred thing as a love of above half a century? People do not mean to be unkind, but it is not kind thus to profane such a friendship as his and mine. . . . . You may assure your friends that nothing has or can come between my deep love for John Henry Newman. As to thinking me pert enough to offer him advice, of course they are welcome enough to believe me capable of any folly."

With the most gratifying expressions of the esteem and approbation of his co-religionists ringing in his ears, Dr. Newman quitted Birmingham, on April 16th, 1879, *en route* for Rome, where the purple was to be conferred upon him with all the form and ceremonial befitting the great occasion. It was announced at the time in an inspired paragraph in the *Times* newspaper, that by the thoughtful consideration of some members of the Catholic nobility adequate provision would be made to enable him to sustain his new dignity. He was accompanied by Fathers Neville and Pope, and other priests of the Oratory. On the 24th he arrived at the Sacred City, the Pope, in consideration of his age and

L

weakness, excusing him from performing the customary formality of going immediately to the Vatican to pay his homage. Three days later he was received at a private audience by the Holy Father, who welcomed him with great kindness and particular consideration. He subsequently visited Cardinal Nina, and went to the English College, St. Peter's, and the Oratory of the Chiesa Nuova. On May 2nd, symptoms of a severe cold appeared, and he was obliged for several days to keep his apartment in the Via Sistina. On the 12th, he went to the residence of Cardinal Howard, in the Palazzo della Pigna, to receive the messenger from the Vatican, bearing the *biglietto* from the Cardinal Secretary of State, informing him that in a secret Consistory held that morning his Holiness had deigned to raise him to the sublime rank of a Cardinal. It was an occasion of great interest and importance. The rooms were crowded with English and American Catholics, ecclesiastics and laymen, members of the Roman nobility, and dignitaries of the Church. Soon after midday the messenger was announced. After the formalities of the occasion were gone through, his Eminence addressed the audience in a speech which manifested all his old felicity of expression and impressive eloquence. "First of all," he said, "I am led to speak of the wonder and profound gratitude which came upon me, and which is still upon me, at the condescension of love towards me of the Holy

Father in signalling me out for so immense an
honour. It was a great surprise. Such an elevation
had never come into my thoughts, and seemed to
be out of keeping with all my antecedents. I had
passed through many trials, but they were over,
and now the end of all things had almost come
to me, and I was at peace. And was it possible
that, after all, I had lived through so many years
for this ? Nor is it easy to say how I could have
borne so great a shock had not the Holy Father
resolved on a second condescension towards me,
which tempered it, and was to all who heard of
it a touching evidence of his kindly and generous
nature. He felt for me, and he told me the
reasons why he had raised me to this high position.
His act, he said, was a recognition of my zeal
and good service for many years in the Catholic
cause. Moreover, he judged it would give pleasure
to English Catholics, and even to Protestant
England if I received some mark of his favour.
After such gracious words from his Holiness I
should have been insensible and heartless if I had
had scruples any longer. In a long course of
years I have made many mistakes. I have nothing
of that high perfection which belongs to the writings
of the Saints—namely, that error could not be found
in them ; but what I trust I may claim throughout
all I have written is this,—an honest intention, an
absence of private ends, a temper of obedience, a
willingness to be corrected, a dread of error, a

desire to serve the Holy Church, and through
Divine mercy a fair share of success." His
Eminence went on to say that to one great
mischief he had from the first opposed himself. For
thirty, forty, fifty years he had resisted, to the best
of his powers, liberalism in the Church; and he
renewed the protest now. "Liberalism in religion,"
he said, "is the doctrine that there is no positive
truth in religion, but that one creed is as good
as another." This was a teaching which was gaining
force daily. People were bent on solving the
problem of securing the submission of the masses
to law and order, without the aid of Christianity.
This "great apostacy" threatened in England a
formidable success. Nevertheless, he had no fear,
for he believed in the ultimate triumph of the
Church over the secular principle. This address,
which was spoken in a strong, clear voice, created
a deep impression upon the new Cardinal's
sympathetic auditors. Dr. Pusey said of it: "It
was a beautiful speech; quite the old John Henry
Newman speaking out the truth, yet not wounding
a single heart." It created considerable sensation
throughout Europe, and not least of all in England.
The first note of the new Cardinal's voice was
sounded in the same key of protest which had
signalised his writings forty years before. At the
end, as at the beginning, he condemned the spirit
of revolt against Authority. In whatever else he
had changed, he had not changed in that. The

days of the Anglican revival and the days of
the Roman Cardinalate were consistent with each
other in this, that alike in both he was the un-
yielding foe of the principles of religious liberalism.

The next day his Eminence received the biretta,
and on the 14th, attended by his trainbearer, gentlemen
of honour in full Pontifical court dress, the Fathers
of the Oratory, and the Master of the Ceremonies
to the Pope, he was received at the door of the
English College, and conducted into a large chamber,
crowded with ladies and gentlemen—Protestants as
well as Catholics—to receive at the hands of the
English-speaking Catholic residents in Rome a
graceful and substantial mark of their regard. The
vestments of his great office, which had been subscribed
for by these admiring co-religionists, were exposed to
view: the cloth of silver cope and jewelled mitre for
state occasions, the pectoral cross and chain, and a
silver-gilt altar candlestick. On each of the vestments
was worked his Eminence's coat-of-arms in proper
heraldic colours, and his motto, *Cor ad cor loquitur*.
The illuminated address, which accompanied this rich
gift and congratulated its recipient on his elevation
to the Sacred Purple, was read by Lady Herbert of
Lea, who had taken an active and zealous part in
organising the testimonial, and in carrying it to a
successful issue. Cardinal Newman warmly and
touchingly thanked his friends for their delicate and
thoughtful kindness, and for their ardent wishes for
his future usefulness. It was announced at the same

time that the Pope had conferred the Church of St. Giorgio in Velabro on him, perhaps choosing it on account of the peculiar fitness of an edifice dedicated to the patron saint of England.

The ceremonial attendant upon the elevation was not, however, yet over. On the 15th, the Pope placed the Red Hat on the heads of the new Cardinals, and afterwards, at a secret Consistory, performed the ceremony of opening and closing their mouths, and giving them their rings. Cardinal Newman was then named a member of four Congregations, those of Rites, of the Propaganda, of Studies, and of Indulgences and Holy Relics. This brought the great business to an end. But the fatigue and excitement of these four consecutive days of ceremony had done their work. The Cardinal had overtaxed his strength. What he had gone through would have tried the endurance of a much younger man. No sooner was it all over than he broke down. Symptoms of what the Romans call *febbre di strapazzo* were observed by his physicians with the utmost anxiety. For many days he lay seriously, if not dangerously, ill. His great age furnished ground for grave uneasiness. Fortunately the febrile symptoms were soon mastered, and then the important task of the doctors was to build up their patient's strength. This they succeeded in doing, to the great joy of the Catholic world, and his Eminence slowly recovered. On June 2nd he went to the Vatican to take his leave of the Pope, and was granted a private audience. The Fathers of the

Oratory were afterwards introduced to His Holiness, who expressed his interest in their work, and his pleasure that the honour conferred upon their illustrious head had given satisfaction to the English public. Having paid a number of farewell visits, Cardinal Newman left Rome on his homeward journey.

He arrived in Birmingham on July 1st, looking very thin and feeble, and accompanied by Father Neville, who had been with him during the whole of his absence, and had tended him most lovingly during his illness. At the Oratory, a large congregation gave him a cordial and reverent welcome. Very touchingly he referred, in a few unstudied words of thanks, to his safe return. " To come home again!" he said, " in that word *home* how much is included. I know well that there is a more heroic life than a home life. We know how the blessed Apostles went about, and we listen to St. Paul's words—those touching words in which he speaks of himself, and says he was an outcast. Then we know, too, that our blessed Lord had not where to lay his head. Therefore, of course, there is a higher life, a more heroic life than that of home. The idea of home is consecrated to us by our patron and founder, St. Philip, for he made the idea of home the very essence of his religion and institute. Therefore, I do indeed feel pleasure in coming home again." And he went on, in a voice faltering with emotion, to say that he had been very ill, and had almost feared that he should never return to England alive, but that he now hoped to spend his days at the Oratory until he was called to the everlasting home. Many of the congregation were moved to tears. The Cardinal himself broke down under the combined effects of physical weakness and mental agitation. It was an affecting, though a happy home-coming. Some of those who were present, and many more who read his remarks the next day, could not help remembering that in the lot which he chose years before, with the courage and honesty of strong convictions, there was no place for the clinging ties of the family circle, for the tender love of woman, or the filial affection of children. But his cloistered life at Edgbaston has been sweetened and refined by the influences of strong friendship, and the spiritual bond which holds the brotherhood at the Oratory together. It has been to him a "home" in a sense which few of us engaged in the hurry and scramble of daily life can understand or attain to. There is something in the apostolic wanderings that claims admiration; and in the life of a modern missionary, passed amid dangers of which we are happily ignorant at home, there is a nobleness of self-denial of which the world takes too little heed; but these are for sanguine youth and lusty manhood. Old age claims its rest; the evening of life should be spent within the shadow of the chimney corner. All who heard Cardinal Newman's contrast between the active life and the home life felt that he, at least, after the heat and burden of the day, was entitled to sit down and rest in the eventide beneath his own vine and fig-tree.

Fresh congratulations awaited him. He had already received and acknowledged an address from the Catholic Archbishop and Bishops of England. Towards the end of July a deputation from the Irish Roman Catholic Union brought him an address, in which reference was made to his efforts for the advancement of University education for Irish Catholics, his lectures on the scope and nature of University education, and the great work he had accomplished, as its Rector, in moulding their newly-formed University. In reply, he said that a desire to serve Ireland was the real motive of his writings and doings while he had been amongst them. The Catholic Total Abstinence League elicited from him the statement that he looked upon them, in the spirit of their work, almost as a religious body. Replying to an address from his own congregation at the Oratory, he said that the Holy Father had expressed a wish that he should not separate himself from his own duties and responsibilities at Edgbaston, and it was therefore a consolation to him to know that he should be there to the end, and should die as he had lived, the Father of the Oratory, and the priest and pastor of the Oratory Mission. Later on, the Duke of Norfolk, the Marquis of Ripon, and other influential mem-

M

bers of the Presentation Fund Committee waited
upon him at Edgbaston and referred, in a eulogistic
address, to his Anglican controversies and their
fruits, his conversion, his University work and the
general distinction, usefulness, and zeal of his life.
Other addresses were presented from the Catholic Poor
Schools' Committee, the Academia, and the Female
College of the Sisters of Notre Dame, Liverpool; to
all of which his Eminence made brief but suitable
replies. One of the most pleasing testimonies of
congratulation came from New South Wales, the
Catholics of which sent him a golden salver and
an appreciatory address.

And here we must leave Cardinal Newman, in
the full enjoyment of "all which should accompany
old age, as honour, love, obedience, troops of
friends." His life, since his elevation to the
Cardinalate, has been singularly uneventful. Now
and then he has made a journey to London to
visit his friend and former pupil, the Duke of
Norfolk, at whose town mansion great receptions of
all that is most eminent in intellect and most distinguished in society had been given in his honour;
or to sit for his portrait to Mr. Ouless or Mr.
Millais, and to have the sad, wistful, far-away look
of those expressive features immortalised on canvas.
Now and then, too, he has officiated at the
consecration of a new church or preached in aid
of some Catholic cause. But for the most part his
days have been spent in study, in quiet contemplation,

and in unobtrusive simplicity. The Prince of the Sacred College has never ceased to be at heart a plain Father of the Oratory. There he lives in the ripeness of a rare old age; vigorous in mind, devout in spirit, and content to know, as some compensation for long years of misconception, that his fellow-countrymen understand him at last, and that even if they differ from him in conclusions, as widely as North differs from South, still they respect his motives and admire his sincerity. There he lives, with the long vista of an eventful career, and the memories of the great incidents in which he has played a part, to fill his retrospective gaze; and the noise of "the mighty waters rolling evermore" to satisfy his imagination as he looks forward to the shores of the "immortal sea."

FINIS.

www.ingramcontent.com/pod-product-compliance
Lightning Source LLC
Chambersburg PA
CBHW031116020726
47495CB00007B/2230